Praise fc

"There's nothing like the smooth storytelling skills of Irene Hannon. She knows how to pace a story as she builds tension and drama and romance. She's a master artist."
—***Best Reads (2010-2021)*** on *Seasons of the Heart*

"Hannon's multithread plot is woven beautifully together to create a tapestry that will enchant romantics of all ages."
—***Publishers Weekly*** on *One Perfect Spring*

"Inspiring prose and embraceable characters…capture the reader from the very first pages."
—***New York Journal of Books*** on *That Certain Summer*

"Touching, compelling, and satisfying."
—***RT Book Reviews*** on *From This Day Forward*

"A great summer read…relatable characters with real-life problems."
—***Radiant Lit*** on *Seaside Reunion*

"A warmhearted journey from loss and guilt to self-forgiveness and love."
—***RT Book Reviews*** on *Once Upon Nantucket*

"A tender and intriguing tale of heartache, loss, and love."
—***Goodreads*** review on *Crossroads*

"An intense, emotional, thought-provoking read."
—***Best Reads (2010-2020)*** on *Child of Grace*

"An exquisite read! A compact love story with all the substance of a longer novel."
—***Amazon*** review on *Second Chance Summer*

"This wonderful story is about accepting that the life God gives can be seen differently when viewed through the eyes of love."
—***RT Book Reviews*** on *Apprentice Father*

"Powerful and compelling."
—***RT Book Reviews*** on *Rainbow's End*

Seasons of the Heart

Family Ties—Book 2
Encore Edition

IRENE HANNON

To my brother, Jim, and his lovely bride, Teresa—
may all your happily-ever-after dreams come true.

Prologue

The car ahead of him was going to crash.

Fingers tightening on the wheel, Dr. Eric Carlson sucked in a breath as the sedan a hundred yards away fishtailed on the icy road, slid sideways off the steep shoulder, and fell out of sight.

The sounds of crunching metal, shattering glass, and screams were masked by the sleet hitting the roof and the volume of the radio Cindy had just cranked up, giving the accident an illusory and distant feel, like an old silent movie.

Yet the tragedy that had just unfolded in front of him was horribly real.

He pressed on the brake and eased to the shoulder, as did two other drivers.

"What are you doing?" Cindy shot him an annoyed look.

"There are people down there who need medical assistance." He reached into the back seat for his bag. Not something most doctors carried these days, but he'd never apologized for being old school. About a lot of things.

"If we stop we'll be late for the reception. Let's just call 911. Those good Samaritans can help." She waved a hand toward the two men who'd emerged from the other cars.

Eric tightened his grip on the bag. Gritted his teeth.

What had happened to the woman he'd married a dozen years ago? Hadn't her heart once been kind and caring? Hadn't

1

she been compassionate and empathetic back then? Hadn't the smiles she'd given him in those early days been tender and warm?

Or had he been so blinded by her beauty that he'd seen only what he'd wanted to see and imagined what had never been there at all?

Who knew?

But he'd taken a vow for better or worse, and he'd stick with it.

Even if it killed him.

"I can't walk away from this, Cindy. I'm a doctor."

"You're a pediatrician, Eric." She didn't say *just*, but her disparaging tone spoke volumes.

He opened his door. "Call 911." Then he stepped into the storm, turned up his collar, and strode toward the embankment, sleet stinging his face much as Cindy's familiar gibe always stung his heart.

When he reached the drop-off, a glance over the edge confirmed the worst.

The car had fallen all the way down the steep hill, perhaps rolling as it plunged, though it had come to rest upright.

He slipped and slid down the precipitous slope and joined the other two motorists who were already beside the vehicle. Both were peering through the windows.

"How many inside?" He angled away from the sleet as a pellet pricked his cheek.

"Two. A man and a woman." One of the men eyed his bag. "Are you a doctor?"

"Yes."

"Lucky for them."

"The woman's conscious, but the guy doesn't look too hot.

The doors are both jammed." The other man frowned.

"Let's see if we can get them open." Eric worked his way around to the passenger side of the car, which was more accessible, and with the three of them tugging they managed to wrench open the battered door.

"Would a flashlight help?" The first guy squinted into the car, the interior shadowy in the fading late-afternoon light.

"Yes. Thanks." While the man began working his way back up the embankment, Eric leaned down and touched the shoulder of the woman passenger. "Ma'am?"

She twisted her head toward him, eyes wide and dazed in a face that belonged in a Raphael painting—a perfect oval, with dark hair and even darker irises.

However, the nasty bump rising on her temple refocused him. Fast. "I'm a doctor. Can you hear me?" He spoke slowly, enunciating each word.

"Yes. I—I'm all right. Except for my arm. But please check on my husband. He's not…he's not responding to me."

He looked past her at the man sprawled behind the steering wheel, his head tipped back, neck fully extended, his seatback almost flat. Blood was seeping from the corner of his mouth, and there was a gash on his forehead. "All right. Try not to move. An ambulance is on the way." He straightened up.

"Are they okay?" The second guy who'd stopped to assist gave him a worried look.

"TBD. Let's see if we can get the other door open."

Between the two of them they managed to pry it back just as the other man returned with a flashlight.

"You want me to point it at the driver?" He wedged himself beside the open door.

"Yes. Thanks."

As the man focused the beam of his light inside, Eric bent down to examine the woman's husband.

Strike one, he wasn't wearing his seat belt.

Strike two, it didn't appear that the side airbag had deployed—if the older model car even had one.

He felt for the man's pulse.

Shallow.

His respiration was also uneven.

Bad news all around.

Without a seat belt, he could have sustained any number of life-threatening injuries, including head-and-neck trauma.

He glanced over at the woman, and fear mushroomed in her eyes at his grim expression.

"He's going to be okay, isn't he? Nothing can happen to him. Not now." A sob caught in her throat, and she reached over to touch her husband's limp arm. "You'll be all right, Jack. I know you will. You have to be."

All at once the man's breathing grew more erratic.

"I need my bag." As Eric barked the words over his shoulder, he fought back a wave of panic. Practicing medicine in an office or a hospital was one thing. Roadside emergency treatment was an entirely different ball game.

When the other motorist returned with his bag, Eric pulled out his stethoscope and put it around his neck.

As he listened to the man's fading pulse, his own heart lost its rhythm.

The paramedics needed to get here. Stat.

But less than thirty seconds later it was clear they weren't going to arrive soon enough. The man's breathing grew more labored as he fought a losing battle to fill his lungs.

Blunt force trauma to the chest was a likely culprit, but the cause didn't matter. The problem needed to be addressed.

Eric reached into his bag again. Pulled out the plastic case containing a pocket mask. Ripped off the protective covering, popped up the valve, and secured the mask to the man's face. Then he began administering rescue breaths.

Didn't help.

The man's breathing faltered. Stopped.

But his pulse continued.

Meaning his airway was blocked, thanks to whatever injuries he'd suffered.

Eric clenched his teeth.

In all his years practicing medicine, he'd never had to open an airway in the field, let alone do it with makeshift lighting and icy sleet peppering the back of his neck.

But if he didn't attempt it tonight, this man was going to die.

Running over cricothyrotomy protocols in his mind, he snapped on a pair of latex gloves. Pulled a cannula from his bag and used his scalpel to cut it to size. Swabbed the man's throat with an antiseptic wipe.

The next part was critical. He had to insert the tube in the right place.

Doing his best not to move the man's neck in case there was an injury to the cervical spine, he felt for the thyroid and cricoid cartilage. Tightening his grip on the scalpel, he immobilized the larynx with the thumb and middle finger of his free hand, then made a cut down the man's throat. Flipped the scalpel over and used the other end to widen the incision. Inserted the cannula into the airway. Watched the man's chest.

After a moment, it rose.

Barely.

But at least he was breathing again.

And hopefully he'd continue to breathe until the emergency responders arrived.

With such a makeshift fix, however, there were no guarantees.

At a strangled sob from the passenger seat, he looked over.

The man's wife was staring at her husband, her face ashen, her breathing shallow and rapid.

She was going into shock.

And he couldn't deal with two patients at once.

Just as panic began to clutch at his windpipe again, the faint wail of a siren pierced the air.

Thank you, God!

Five tense, endless minutes later a paramedic joined him. In a few clipped sentences he brought the man up to speed, then turned over the patients to the emergency pros.

"Lucky for this guy you were here." The paramedic eased in and took over. "Thanks for stopping. Immediate medical attention can make all the difference in trauma situations, as you know."

"I was happy to help." He backed off, climbed up the embankment, and thanked the other two motorists for their help. Then he gave a statement to the police.

But before he returned to his car, he glanced back down at the scene, now surrealistically illuminated by the strobing lights from the emergency vehicles.

The woman was standing, cradling one arm, and though it was clear the paramedic was urging her to sit, she was shaking her head as she watched the other two technicians extricate her husband from the battered car. Even from a distance, her fear was almost palpable.

And for just a moment, despite the man's traumatic injuries,

Eric envied him. His wife's love had been evident in her eyes, her expression, her very body language. It was clear her husband was the center of her world. Which was as it should be in a good marriage.

But it wasn't how Cindy would look at him if they were in a similar situation.

Gut twisting, he turned away and walked back to his car. To the wife who put up with him for what he could provide but whose love had lapsed long ago.

If it had ever been there.

And she wasn't going to be happy about tonight's delay, even if he'd saved a man's life.

But saving a physical life wasn't saving a lifestyle. And in all likelihood, the road ahead wouldn't be easy for either that man or his wife. Tonight could very well be only the beginning of their trauma.

And as he reached the car and opened the door, he acknowledged a sad truth.

Maybe Cindy had been right after all.

Maybe he should just have driven on.

1

"**M**rs. Nolan, the doctor will see Sarah now."

Kate glanced up from the book she was reading to her daughter and smiled. "All right. Thanks." She slung her purse over her shoulder and stood, reaching down to take Sarah's hand. "Come on, honey. It's time to go in."

"Do I have to?"

Sending the nurse a silent apology for the delay, she dropped to one knee beside Sarah. "You don't want to have those nasty tummy aches anymore, do you, honey? The doctor can help make them go away. And I'll stay with you the whole time. I promise."

A tear brimmed on Sarah's lower lash, and she sniffed. "I don't like doctors."

"You used to like Dr. Davis, remember? And this doctor is a friend of his. So I'm sure you'll like him too."

"He's not going to give me a shot, is he?"

"I don't think so. Not today." She pulled her into a quick hug and stood again, fighting back the familiar rush of fear that threatened to swamp her whenever her daughter caught so much as the sniffles.

What would she do if something serious was wrong with this child of her heart, who filled her life with joy and meaning and gave her someone to love?

8

The answer was simple.

She'd curl up and die.

But she should put aside those kinds of negative thoughts. Sarah would be fine. She had to be.

Except there was no guarantee of that, as she knew all too well. Everything didn't always turn out fine, no matter how much you wished it would or how hard you prayed for a happy ending.

They followed the nurse to an examining room, where the woman ushered them in. "The doctor will be with you in a few minutes."

"Shall I undress Sarah?" Kate guided her inside while Sarah maintained a death grip on her hand.

The woman sized up Sarah's shorts and knit top. "I don't think that will be necessary. That outfit should make it easy for the doctor to check her out."

Once the woman exited, Kate sat and tried to coax her lips into a cheery smile. "Shall we finish our story?" She held up the book she'd brought to pass the time in the waiting room.

"Okay." Sarah climbed onto her lap.

Though her daughter quickly became engrossed in the fanciful tale, Kate's mind was only half on the words she was reading. It was bad enough when Sarah got a simple case of the sniffles, but what could be causing the mysterious ache in her daughter's stomach?

Hopefully this new doctor would be able to answer that question.

When a brief knock interrupted her reading a few minutes later, she took a steadying breath, closed the book, and looked up as the door swung open.

A tall, trim, vaguely familiar man with hair the color of sun-ripened wheat and intense blue eyes stood on the other side.

She'd seen him somewhere before. Of that she was certain. Yet hard as she tried, she couldn't place him.

Based on the flicker of recognition in his eyes, he'd made a connection too. But his professional smile didn't waver as he held out his hand. Nor did he suggest they'd met before when he greeted her.

"Mrs. Nolan? I'm Eric Carlson."

Kate returned his firm grip. "Nice to meet you, Doctor."

"And this must be the patient." He dropped to the balls of his feet beside her daughter, who was watching him with a wary expression, finger in mouth. "Hello, Sarah. I'm Dr. Eric." When she didn't respond, he tried again. "You know, I have a big tank of beautiful fish in my office you might like to see after we're finished. What's your favorite color?"

Slowly she removed her finger. "Pink."

"Well, I happen to have a bright pink fish in there. Would you like to see it later?"

She studied him for a moment. "Are you going to give me a shot?"

His lips twitched. "Nope. No shots today. But I'd like to look in your ears and peek at your tonsils if that's okay. And I'll let you listen to my heart if you let me listen to yours."

"Okay, I guess." When Sarah glanced at her, Kate offered an encouraging smile and nod.

"Then let's get this show on the road so you can go see my fish." He stood, picked her up, then settled her on the end of the table.

From that point on, the exam proceeded smoothly. The doctor even elicited a giggle or two from her daughter.

Amazing how he managed to put her shy, reserved little girl at ease.

As he worked, he threw a few astute, specific questions over his shoulder to her, never shifting his focus from Sarah. When he finished, he straightened up and smiled down at his patient. "That wasn't too bad, was it?"

"No. It didn't hurt at all. And you're nice."

"Best compliment I've had all day." He winked and swung her to the floor, then bent down to retrieve a wayward cotton ball.

A jolt of recognition rippled through Kate.

Maybe it was his motion of leaning close to her, or the position of his body in conjunction to hers, or the way the overhead lighting drew out the burnished gold in his hair. But with sudden, startling clarity his identity clicked into place.

This was the doctor who'd leaned over in exactly the same way as he'd worked on Jack in their wrecked car five years before.

At her sharp intake of breath, the pediatrician looked over at her. Searched her face. Then, with a smile that seemed a bit forced, he shifted his attention to Sarah. "Are you ready to see that pink fish now?"

She nodded. "It's all right, isn't it, Mommy?"

Somehow Kate found her voice. "Yes."

Eric took Sarah's hand and spoke over her head. "I'll be back in a minute."

As the two of them exited, Kate continued processing the bizarre coincidence. When her own pediatrician had retired a few weeks ago, all she'd done was select the most geographically convenient replacement from the list he'd provided.

Eric Carlson.

The man who'd saved Jack's life.

The man she'd always intended to identify, track down, and thank.

But she'd never followed through. The demands of her life after the accident had been overwhelming. It had taken every ounce of her energy just to make it through each day.

Yet now, thanks to this chance encounter, she'd finally have a chance to say a long overdue thank you.

* * *

Eric paused outside the treatment room. Filled his lungs.

What a strange coincidence that his new patient's mother was the same woman who'd been in the smashed car that harrowing night five years ago.

And she'd recognized him, just as he'd recognized her.

Odd that she'd remember him, given all the trauma of that night, but he'd never forgotten her Madonna-like face—even if her beauty was tempered now with worry and fatigue. The fine lines at the corners of her eyes and the dark smudges beneath them gave mute testimony to a life of unrelenting strain, and her eyes reflected disillusion and sadness instead of the love that had filled them on that fateful night.

Whatever burden she'd carried since the accident had taken a toll.

Maybe, with a few discreet questions, she'd give him a clue about that. Assuage the curiosity that sometimes surfaced in his quiet moments about what had become of her and her husband.

Calling up a smile, he reentered the room, shut the door, and took a seat. "I left Sarah in my office with one of my assistants. She'll keep her occupied until we're finished."

"You were the doctor at the accident, weren't you?"

So much for diplomatically leading up to that subject.

"Yes. I recognized you the minute I came in the door."

"It took a few minutes longer for your identity to register with me. And I owe you an apology. I never said thank you, even though I meant to."

"No thanks were necessary. I'm a doctor. Helping sick or injured people is my job."

She shook her head. "No. You didn't have to stop. A lot of people would have driven by rather than get involved, especially in that kind of weather." Her throat worked as she swallowed. "I don't remember much about that night. I had a slight concussion and a broken arm, and everything has always been a blur. But they told me later that you saved Jack's life. I always intended to find out your name and let you know I appreciated your help."

He waved that off. "All I did was open an airway. It was enough to give him a fighting chance until he got to the hospital." He flicked a glance at the ring on her left hand before proceeding carefully. "From what I could tell, your husband's condition was very serious."

"It was. Two vertebrae in his neck were crushed and he had severe head injuries. At first they weren't sure he'd even make it through the night. But somehow he held on. One day became two. Then a week. Then a month. I never gave up hope, despite his poor prognosis. The doctors said even if he came out of his coma, he'd be paralyzed." She exhaled, and when she continued her voice was laced with pain. "But that ended up being a moot point. He died seven months later without ever regaining consciousness."

Eric's stomach bottomed out.

That was exactly what he'd feared might happen.

"I'm sorry." Inadequate, but there were no words to ease the burden of grief or the devastating sense of emptiness and loss that accompanied the death of a loved one.

She blinked away the sheen in her eyes. "Thank you. You'd

think after more than four years I'd be able to handle the loss better than this, but Jack and Sarah were my whole world. Sarah was only six weeks old when it happened, and we had so many plans, so much to look forward to." She dipped her chin. Drew a shaky breath. "Everyone said that in time life would feel normal again. But it didn't. When a tragedy like that happens, you never get over it. You just get on with it."

Pressure built in Eric's throat. "It takes a lot of courage just to do that."

She shook her head. "It doesn't take courage to do what you have to do. Sarah needs me, and I love her with all my heart. That's why these mysterious stomach pains have me so worried."

While he couldn't change the tragedy that had brought Kate more than her share of heartache, at least he could set her mind at ease about her daughter. "I don't think you have any worries about those in terms of her physical condition, Mrs. Nolan. She seems like a very healthy little girl."

"Then what's the problem?"

"Has there been any recent trauma in her life?"

"Yes. My mother died suddenly a month ago."

Another death in the family?

How much loss was one woman supposed to take?

"I'm sorry."

"Thank you. Mom and Sarah were close. We all were. Sort of like The Three Musketeers."

"Coping with the loss of a beloved grandmother would be tough on a child Sarah's age."

"Especially since Mom lived with us and watched Sarah for me during the school year while I taught. I had to find day care for her on the fly, and she started a couple of weeks ago, right before I went back to school. It's been a big adjustment for both of us. I hate leaving her with strangers because she tends to be shy. And I'm afraid she may not be mixing well with the other children." Her voice caught.

He frowned. "That background further supports my theory that her stomach pains have an emotional rather than physical basis. The loss of her grandmother coupled with being thrust into a new day care situation would cause a huge upheaval in her life. Are there any other options?"

"No. And the place she goes wasn't my first choice. But it was the best I could do on short notice. Most day-care facilities are booked solid and have waiting lists a mile long." She sighed. "I wish I could have found a home-based setting."

He gentled his voice. "You're doing the best you can under difficult circumstances. Don't be too hard on yourself."

Gratitude warmed her eyes. As if she was in desperate need of reassurance and support. "Thank you again. But it's not good enough." She kneaded the bridge of her nose. "I'll just have to keep looking."

As he studied the furrows on her brow, an idea began to take shape in his mind.

It was kind of off the wall, but if he could make it happen several problems would be solved in one fell swoop. Sarah would have more personal day care. Her mother would have more peace of mind. And he'd have some relief from the constant worry in his own life.

Until—or unless—he worked out the details, however, it was best not to raise expectations.

"I know this is a difficult time for you and Sarah, but remember that children are resilient. You're clearly a caring, conscientious parent, and children know when they're loved. That makes a huge difference. I'd suggest giving her a little extra TLC, and if the stomach problem persists I can refer you to a counselor for her."

The corners of her mouth rose a hair. "You have an excellent bedside manner, Doctor—even if I'm not the patient. I feel much calmer."

He returned her smile. "I'm glad. Let me know if Sarah continues to have problems, but I think she'll adjust in time."

"I hope so. And I'll keep searching for another day-care option."

Eric let that pass as he stood, then ushered her to the door and down the hall to retrieve her daughter.

A more personal situation would be best for the grieving little girl, no question about it.

And if everything went as he hoped, Kate's wish for that very thing just might come true.

* * *

"You want me to do *what?*"

As his mother stared at him, her glass of orange juice frozen halfway to her mouth, Eric shifted in his seat at the table for two he'd snagged at their favorite after-church Sunday breakfast spot.

No surprise that she was shocked by his suggestion. Mom had become a hermit since Dad died six months ago. Again, no surprise there either, considering she was a nurturer at heart and now had no one to nurture. While she'd given Dad the best possible care after his health began to fail a couple of years ago, she now felt useless.

Which was why the idea he'd had in the office a couple of days ago seemed like the perfect solution for everyone. His mother needed someone to take care of. Sarah needed someone to watch her. Kate needed the peace of mind that a good caregiver would provide. And he wanted to help his mother find new purpose in life.

It was an ideal arrangement.

But from the way Mom was staring at him, you'd think he'd suggested she take up skydiving.

"I'd like you to consider watching one of my patients five days a week during school hours while her mother teaches." He took a sip of his own juice.

His mother set her glass down and continued to gape at him. "Why on earth would I want to do that?"

Eric waited until the server set their plates in front of them before responding. "She needs help, Mom."

His mother narrowed her eyes. "Who? The mother or the little girl?"

"Both."

At least he'd aroused her curiosity. Mom hadn't looked this interested in anything since before Dad died. During the Sunday breakfasts that had become a ritual over the past six months, she was usually subdued and picked at her food. Today he'd managed to snap her out of her apathy, if only for a few moments.

In fact, as she studied him her expression reminded him of the probing look she'd always given him during his growing-up years when she was trying to figure out what was going on in his head.

Her next question confirmed his take. "In all the years you've been a doctor, I've never seen you take such a personal interest in a patient. Is there something you're not telling me about this situation?"

She was as sharp and insightful as ever.

Meaning it would be smart to come clean.

17

"As a matter of fact, yes." He gave her a quick recap of the scene that had played out in his office and filled her in on the accident from five years ago that he'd never shared with her.

"Strange that your paths suddenly crossed again." She gave him a shrewd appraisal.

"Very."

"Despite the odd coincidence, though, there's no reason for you to get involved in this woman's life, is there? You must meet a lot of parents who are facing similar dilemmas."

He couldn't argue with that. Broken families, single-parent households, problem stepchildren—he'd seen it all. And he'd never before been tempted to intervene on a personal level. At least not to this extent.

Mom was right.

There wasn't any reason for him to get involved in Kate Nolan's life.

Except he wanted to. And at the moment he wasn't inclined to analyze why.

"Let's just say I think it would be the charitable thing to do." He kept his tone conversational. "You have the time. She has the need. It's the right combination of circumstances at the right time. There's nothing more to it than that."

Despite her skeptical expression, his mother didn't belabor the point. Instead, she poked at her scrambled eggs and pursed her lips.

Eric waited in silence. He wouldn't push her if she wasn't willing to give this a try, but he knew in his gut the arrangement would reap benefits for all involved.

At last she met his gaze, her own troubled. "I don't know, Eric. It's a big responsibility. And they're strangers to me. What if we don't like each other?"

"You'll like them, Mom. Guaranteed. And they'll love you.

Sarah misses her grandmother, and I can't think of a better surrogate. You were made for that role."

And this was the only chance she'd have to play it.

The unspoken words hung in the air between them.

His marriage had produced no children, and there wouldn't be another walk down the aisle. He'd made his peace with that, even if his mom hadn't.

As her next comment proved.

"I haven't given up on having a real grandchild, you know."

"It's time you did."

"You're only thirty-eight, Eric. It's not too late to have a family."

"Mom."

She ignored the subtle warning in his tone. "Of course, you'd need a wife first."

"I have a wife."

"You've been divorced for almost five years, Eric."

"You know how I feel about that."

Anna sighed. Eyed the wedding band on his left hand. "Yes. Till death do us part. But you tried to salvage your marriage. It wasn't your fault Cindy wouldn't agree to counseling. And I can't believe God would want you to spend the rest of your life alone."

Maybe not. And maybe his attitude was archaic in this day and age of high divorce rates.

But as far as he was concerned, marriage vows were sacred, and they were for life. Even if Cindy had remarried four years ago.

Besides, his dedication to his career had ruined one marriage. How could he in good conscience inflict that burden on another woman?

And they'd wandered far from the subject at hand. It was

time to get back on track.

"None of this has any bearing on our discussion, Mom. If you're worried about whether you'll all get along, I could call Kate Nolan, see if she's interested, and arrange for her to stop by and visit you if she is. That way, the two of you can size each other up and you can meet Sarah. How does that sound?"

"I suppose I could consider it. But I'm not making any promises, Eric."

"I don't expect you to."

She forked a bite of her eggs. "I do feel sorry for her, though. So many burdens on someone so young. How old did you say Sarah was when the accident happened?"

"Six weeks."

His mother shook her head. "I can't even imagine trying to cope with that. It's challenging enough for two people to raise a child. But for a single working mother, it would be twice as hard. And then to lose her own mother so recently." Mom tut-tutted. "She does sound like she needs help."

"She does. She's been living under tremendous strain for years. I'd say she's approaching the danger level on the stress scale."

"Well, it can't hurt to meet her. And if we click, I suppose I could help her out until she finds someone to take over on a permanent basis."

The tension in his shoulders began to ease. "I know she'd appreciate it, Mom."

"This is all contingent on whether we get along, though."

"You'll get along fine."

"How can you be so sure?"

"Because I know you."

"But you don't know Kate Nolan. You just met her."

"Let's just call it intuition."

Thankfully, his mother seemed to accept that explanation…even if it wasn't quite true. Because for whatever reason, he felt as if he *did* know Kate Nolan.

And that was a puzzle he didn't intend to tackle while he ate his eggs.

2

K ate pulled to a stop in front of the small, tidy brick bungalow and took a slow, steadying breath.

This was bizarre.

Eric Carlson's call to check on Sarah two days ago had been impressive enough. How many doctors ever followed up personally after an office visit? But his suggestion that his mother might be the solution to her day-care problem had been mind-blowing—even after he'd explained that the arrangement would be as beneficial to his mom as it would be to Sarah and her.

While that might be true, as far as she was concerned *she* was the one who had the most to gain—if everything worked out.

Which she was about to find out.

As she opened her car door, the stifling heat and humidity of the St. Louis summer slammed against her with a force that almost took her breath away. It was a bit late in the season for such sauna-like conditions, but then again, in St. Louis you never knew. It was too bad the weather had decided to act up today, though. Recess duty at school had left her wilted and drained. On top of that, Sarah was cranky after another unpleasant session at the day care center.

Bottom line, this wasn't an ideal time to make a positive first impression.

But it was too late to change the appointment now.

"Come on, honey, it will be cool in the house." She opened the back door, unbuckled Sarah's seat belt, and reached for her hand.

"I want to go home." Sarah pressed harder into the booster seat.

"I know. So do I. But I promised Dr. Eric we'd stop and visit his mommy. She's lonesome here all by herself. And we wouldn't want to break our promise to Dr. Eric, would we?"

Apparently Sarah wasn't in the mood for logic or guilt trips. Instead of responding, she clamped her lips together and folded her arms.

Kate's head began to pound. "We won't stay long. But I promised Dr. Eric we'd stop by. We have to go in." She struggled to keep her voice calm as she extracted her protesting daughter from the seat.

"I don't want to!" Sarah thrashed, in full resistance mode.

"Sarah! Stop whining and stop fighting me." Kate's patience evaporated. "We're going to go in. Now. And we'll be done faster if you cooperate." Taking her hand in a firm grip, she towed her foot-dragging daughter toward the front door.

Sarah continued to whimper as they made their way up the brick walkway, and despite her terse tone of moments before Kate could empathize. After today's heat and the stress of the past few weeks, she felt like doing exactly the same thing.

Instead, she forced herself to pay attention to her surroundings.

Anna Carlson's home was sheltered by large trees and had a fenced backyard that would provide a shady, secure space for a child to run and play. And it was just ten minutes from her apartment.

Perfect.

23

Assuming this worked out.

As Kate pressed the doorbell, she glanced down at her daughter. Sarah still looked hot and unhappy and ill-tempered. She could only hope that once inside, where it was cool, she'd settle down and give Eric's mother a glimpse of the charming little girl she usually was.

The door was pulled open, and Kate took a quick inventory of the woman on the other side, who bore no resemblance to Eric. Her hair was mostly gray, though traces of faded auburn revealed its original color—a marked contrast to Eric's sandy-hued hair. While Eric had to be close to six feet tall, his mother was about five-four at the most. And unlike Eric, who had a trim, athletic build, his mother was softly rounded.

But she had a pleasant face, and her eyes were kind.

"You must be Kate." The older woman smiled.

"Yes. And this is Sarah." She tugged her daughter from behind her back.

Anna's smile widened as Sarah gave her a wary once-over. "My! You're much more grown-up than I expected. I'm so glad you and your mommy decided to visit me today. It's always nice to make new friends, isn't it? Why don't you both come in before you melt?"

She moved aside, and Kate stepped into the welcome coolness. Sighed. "It feels wonderful in here."

"Yes, it does. Air conditioning is one of those blessings we tend to take for granted." Anna led them into the living room. "Let me get you both something to help you cool off."

"We don't want to be a bother." Kate sat on the couch, Sarah glued to her side.

"It's no bother at all." She looked at Sarah. "I bet you're the kind of girl who likes ice cream. Am I right?" At Sarah's cautious nod, a fan of lines appeared beside Anna Carlson's eyes. "That's what I thought. And I have a whole carton of chocolate chip in the freezer."

Sarah stopped fidgeting. "That's my favorite."

"Mine too. If it's okay with your mother, I'll get you a big bowl. Kate?"

"Fine by me."

"Wonderful." She refocused on Sarah. "Would you like to come out to the kitchen with me? I have a parakeet you might like to meet."

Sarah's brow puckered. "What's a para—parakeet?"

"A very beautiful bird. Sometimes he even talks. His name is George. Would you like to see him?"

Kate angled toward Sarah and gave her an encouraging smile. "Why don't you take a look?"

After a moment, Sarah rose. "I've never seen a talking bird."

"Then we'll have to try to get George to talk to you." Eric's mother motioned toward the back of the house. "I'll get Sarah settled in the kitchen with her ice cream, and then we can have a chat, Kate. Would you like a glass of iced tea?"

"That would be great. Thank you."

When Anna started toward the kitchen, Sarah fell in beside her. "What does George say?"

"Oh, lots of things. His favorite expression is, "'Looking good, cutie.'"

Sarah giggled. "What color is he?"

"Green and yellow. And he has black lines on his head and his wings that…"

As the two of them disappeared into the kitchen and their voices faded away, the knot in Kate's stomach began to loosen.

Sarah's quick warm-up to Eric's mother was encouraging.

The ability to befriend children must run in the Carlson family.

While she listened to the animated but muted chatter coming from the kitchen, she gave the living room a slow sweep. It was a cozy space, neat as a pin but not too fussy. The furniture was comfortable and overstuffed, made for sitting in, not admiring from afar. Fresh flowers stood in a vase on the coffee table, and family photos were arranged on the mantel.

She rose and moved closer to examine them, starting at one end with a black-and-white wedding photo of Eric's parents. Next was a picture of the same couple cutting a twenty-fifth-anniversary cake. In that one it was clear where Eric got his looks. His father was tall, dignified, blond, and blue-eyed. In other words, an older version of Eric.

The rest of the photos featured Eric. As a baby. In a cub scout uniform. In a cap and gown, flanked by his proud parents. On the deck of a cruise ship as an adult, again with his parents. And on the wall next to the mantel, a framed newspaper clipping about Eric being named man of the year by a local charitable organization held a place of honor.

Clearly, he was his parents' pride and joy.

But there was something missing from this gallery.

Namely, photos of Eric and his wife.

And he *was* married, given the wedding band that had caught her eye in his office.

So why weren't there any photos to indicate he had a wife or family? Or that he ever had?

Curious.

As his mother reentered the room, Kate swiveled away from the mantel, warmth creeping across her cheeks. "I hope you don't mind me admiring your pictures."

"Not at all." She deposited a tray holding glasses of iced tea and a plate of cookies on the coffee table. "That's what they're there for. Now, why don't we relax and have a chat? Sarah is trying to get George to talk, and I also left her with crayons and paper and asked her to draw me a picture of him. That should keep her busy for a few minutes."

"You and your son both have a way with children, Mrs. Carlson." Kate returned to her seat.

"It's Anna. And it's not hard to bond with a lovely little girl like Sarah."

Kate grimaced. "She wasn't so lovely a few minutes ago. More like cranky and belligerent. I almost had to drag her in here. I figured you'd take one look and send us packing. I think she had a rough session at day care."

"Eric tells me that until your mother passed away a month ago, she watched Sarah. I'm so very sorry, my dear. The loss of a mother is one of life's greatest trials."

At the empathy and compassion in the older woman's voice, Kate's throat thickened. With all the turmoil since Mom's death, she'd had little time to grieve. But the ache of loss was heavy in her heart.

"Thank you. Mom and I were always close, but during these past few years since she came to live with us we forged an even stronger bond. My dad died about eight years ago, and Mom sold the farm in Ohio where we grew up and moved to an apartment in Cincinnati. She came to help out when Jack was injured, and after he died she stayed on. It was the best possible arrangement for all of us under the circumstances."

"You must miss her very much."

"I do. It was hard enough when Jack died, but Mom was there for me to lean on. Now it's just me and Sarah. I stay in close touch with my sister in Tennessee, but it's not the same as having an in-person chat."

"No. Nothing takes the place of the physical presence of the people we love. But I'm sure Sarah brings you great joy."

"Yes, she does. More so because she was an unexpected gift. My husband and I tried for years to start a family and had almost given up when we discovered I was pregnant. I couldn't wait to be a full-time mom, and my husband was one hundred percent supportive of that."

Funny.

She'd never shared much about that decision with anyone, but Anna was easy to talk to.

"Kudos to you both. So many young mothers try to have it all. Not that you can't, of course. I just don't think you can have it all at the same time. As the Good Book says, 'To everything there is a season.' I'm a firm believer that children need a full-time mother unless there are extraordinary circumstances."

"I agree. But as it turned out, I was faced with those extraordinary circumstances. I assume Eric told you what happened."

"He filled me in on the basics. I understand you lost your husband shortly after Sarah was born."

Kate took a slow breath. Smoothed out a wrinkle in her slacks. "Yes. The accident happened on our first night out together after Sarah was born. We'd had an early dinner to celebrate our anniversary."

Shock flattened Anna's features. "Oh, my dear. I had no idea. How awful."

She swallowed. "Everything about our life changed that day forever. Long-term care is expensive, and insurance doesn't cover everything, so after Jack died I went back to teaching, sold our house, and moved into an apartment. Somehow I managed to keep going, but when Mom died everything fell apart again." Her voice hiccupped, and she paused. Struggled to hang on to her composure.

Anna reached out and laid her hand over her fingers. "You've had more than your share of trials."

"And the latest is Sarah." Her words came out shaky, and she took a slow breath. "Seeing her so unhappy at day care is tearing me up. I need to find a more personal situation with someone who can give her the love and affection and attention I'd give her if I could be there. Your son thought you might be willing to pinch-hit, at least until I can find a more permanent arrangement. I'm hoping you are." Because after watching Eric's mother and Sarah bond, after seeing the woman's welcoming home and child-friendly backyard, and after being treated to the older woman's gracious empathy, it was clear this would be an answer to her prayers.

Anna set her iced tea glass on a coaster, faint creases denting her brow. "I'd like to help you, my dear. But you do understand that I'm not experienced in day care, don't you?"

"You're a mother. And you raised a fine son, from what I can see. You seem kind and caring, and Sarah took to you immediately. Those are solid credentials as far as I'm concerned."

"Well, I suppose I should take advantage of this opportunity to play grandmother, since Eric has made it clear it might be my one and only chance."

Kate took a sip of her tea.

Since Anna had put the subject on the table, why not ask the question it raised—and perhaps satisfy her curiosity about why there were no photos of Eric's wife on the mantel?

"Why would this be your only chance?"

"Eric's divorced. Has been for almost five years. He and Cindy never had any children. Pity too, when he loves children so much."

"He could remarry."

"Not Eric. If he takes a vow, he sticks with it."

Admirable.

"Well, I think I can safely say that Sarah would love being your surrogate granddaughter."

Anna's lips flexed. "I suppose I shouldn't look a gift horse in the mouth."

"Does that mean you'll watch her?"

"Yes. At least for a while. Why don't you fill me in on the schedule you're thinking about?"

Within ten minutes the details were settled, and Kate felt as if a burden had been lifted from her shoulders. "I can't ever thank you enough for this."

"I'm glad I can help. It seems like you've had far too many tribulations for someone so young."

"To tell you the truth, I don't feel very young these days. I may be only thirty-six, but sometimes I feel ancient."

Sarah burst into the room to show off her drawing of George, putting an end to the adult exchange, and as Anna exclaimed over the artwork, Kate settled back with her iced tea.

Once upon a time, Eric had saved her husband's life.

Now Kate felt as if he'd saved hers as well.

And for that she owed him a debt of gratitude she could never begin to repay.

* * *

"So how did it go?" Eric leaned back in his office chair, cell to ear.

"I'm fine, thanks. How are you?"

At his mother's gently chiding response, he rubbed the back of his neck. "Sorry. Your meeting with Mrs. Nolan was on my mind all afternoon, and this is the first chance I've had to call."

"It's seven-thirty. You must have had a busy day."

"I did. I had an emergency at the hospital that delayed me."

"Why don't you follow the example of most of your colleagues and turn over your patients' care to a pediatric hospitalist while they're in the hospital?"

The same question Cindy used to ask.

And he gave his mom the same answer.

"Because I'm old school. And it's comforting to patients and parents to see a familiar face in that intimidating setting."

She huffed. "You work too hard, Eric. Especially since the divorce. I admire your dedication, but you need to have a life too."

They'd been over this before, countless times.

And his mom was right.

The truth was, after Cindy left and he'd decided marriage and medicine didn't mix, he'd immersed himself in his work to the exclusion of just about everything else. That wasn't healthy. He needed to back off from some of his commitments, resign from a couple of the boards he was on, and give serious thought to his partner's suggestion that they bring another doctor into their practice.

He'd do all that too—as soon as he had a spare minute.

In the meantime, however, the stress level of one beautiful but sad mother and her little girl were front and center in his mind.

"You're changing the subject, Mom."

"I worry about you."

"Worry about Mrs. Nolan and Sarah instead. They need it more than I do."

"For the immediate future, you may be right. And our

meeting went well. Sarah is a precious, sensitive child, and I can see how she'd feel lost in one of those big day care centers. As for Kate… Oh, dear, that poor woman. What a tragic story. To have that accident happen on her wedding anniversary—I can't begin to imagine the horror."

His hand tightened on his cell.

Neither could he, not after the love he'd seen reflected in her eyes in the crumpled car as she'd looked at her critically injured husband.

"I didn't know about the significance of the date."

"It had to be terrible. Anyway, she looked so lost and alone when we talked that I wanted to hug her."

He could relate. The same inappropriate urge had swept over him in the office the day she'd told him her story. "Did you agree to watch Sarah?"

"How could I refuse after hearing everything they'd been through? Besides, I liked them both. It won't be a hardship. Kate wanted to pay me far too much, but I got her down to a reasonable amount."

His lips quirked. "I think bargaining is supposed to work the other way around."

"There are extenuating circumstances. I got the feeling cash flow is a problem—and I don't need the money."

Warmth filled his heart. "How did I get lucky enough to have you for a mother?"

"The feeling is mutual. Anyway, Sarah will start coming tomorrow."

Eric blinked. "That's fast."

"Why wait? My schedule is open, and Kate can't get her daughter out of that place fast enough. Of course, I had to run to the store and pick up a few things. Peanut butter and jelly, ingredients for my sugar cookies, coloring books, Play-Doh. I'm not used to entertaining a child." There was new energy in his mom's voice, an enthusiasm that had been missing for months.

Apparently his instinct that this arrangement would be beneficial for everyone had been spot-on.

"Do you want me to do anything?"

"No. I have it under control, thanks."

"In that case, I'll see you Sunday, as usual. And good luck."

"Thanks. I think this will work out fine. Talk to you soon."

As they rang off, Eric leaned back in his chair, feeling more upbeat than he had in a long while.

Because he'd done a good deed for his mom, Kate, and Sarah, of course. The sudden lift in his spirits had nothing to do with the fact that this arrangement would give him an opportunity to see Sarah's beautiful mother again.

You sure about that, Carlson?

At the little voice in his head, he frowned. Pushed himself to his feet.

Yeah, he was sure. Been there, done that.

Even if he wasn't still married, he'd learned the hard lesson that marriage and medicine didn't mix. At least not for him.

And while that had been a bitter pill to swallow, he was cured.

Going forward, the solo life was his lot.

End of story.

* * *

"You know, one of these days I'm going to stop inviting you, since you never come, but Mary said I should try one more time. So…Labor Day weekend barbecue, Saturday, five o'clock. What's your excuse this time?"

As his partner cornered him in the break room at their office, Eric refilled his coffee mug.

Since they'd clicked during their residency days, he'd loved Frank like a brother. They saw eye to eye on substantive issues, enjoyed each other's company, and respected each other's skills.

He had just one complaint.

Frank had made it his mission to spice up his partner's almost nonexistent social life.

In general, Eric deflected those efforts...but why not throw his friend a curve today, since he had no other plans for the holiday weekend?

"No excuse. I'll be there." He took a sip of his coffee.

Frank did a double take. "You mean you'll come?"

"Yes."

"Well, hallelujah! Wait till I tell Mary our persistence finally paid off."

"Can I bring anything?"

"Nothing except a date." Frank grinned.

He was joking, of course. His partner knew he never dated.

But all at once an image of Kate Nolan flashed through Eric's mind.

If ever a woman needed a lighthearted, no-strings evening, it was her.

And if she agreed to go with him, Frank might stop trying to fix his social life.

Hmm.

Could be a win/win all around.

Frank cocked his head, like a hound on the scent of its quarry. "Are you actually thinking about bringing someone?"

He angled sideways. Added a bit more cream to his coffee.

"Maybe." He pulled a napkin from the holder on the counter.

When he risked a peek at his partner, Frank's jaw had dropped.

Before the other man could follow up, Eric strode toward the door. "On to the next patient."

Lips twitching, he continued down the hall.

It had been fun to pull the rug out from someone who thought he was so predictable.

But it wasn't as funny three days later. Because he had yet to summon up the courage to call Kate. And if he didn't show up with a date, Frank would badger him about the mystery woman he'd hinted he might bring.

Even worse?

If his partner now thought he was willing to start dating, he'd renew his efforts to set him up, as he had relentlessly for a year or two after the divorce.

Stifling a groan, Eric settled on a stool in his kitchen and closed his eyes.

Unless he wanted his friend and colleague to step in and try to fill the gap in his social life, he better show up at the barbecue with someone.

And Kate Nolan was the only option. That's why he'd already laid the groundwork to free her up for the evening.

Palms sweating, he picked up his cell phone and tapped in her number.

Three rings in, she answered with a tentative greeting. As if she expected this to be a crank call or solicitation.

Not surprising, since a call from his personal number would show up as an unknown ID on her screen.

"Mrs. Nolan? It's Eric Carlson."

A few beats passed.

"Hello, Doctor. This is a surprise."

"I, uh, wanted to thank you for your note." It might be best to start off with an expression of appreciation for the warm, heart-felt letter she'd sent to his office after his mother agreed to watch Sarah.

"It was the least I could do. But you didn't have to bother calling me."

Hearing her voice was no bother—but he left that unsaid.

"I also wanted to tell you how glad I am that the arrangement with my mom seems to be working out. She's much more like her old self, even though it's only been a week."

"Likewise for Sarah. This seems like a match made in heaven. She and your mom hit it off from the beginning. Sarah's morning tune has changed from 'Do I have to go?' to 'Hurry up, Mom. We'll be late for Aunt Anna's.' In fact, I'm not sure how she'll manage away from your mom for three whole days over the Labor Day holiday."

The perfect opening.

"Maybe she doesn't have to."

"What do you mean?" Kate sounded puzzled.

Eric took a deep breath and pressed a finger against a stray crumb on the counter. "I know this is a bit last-minute, but my partner is having a barbecue Saturday night, and I thought it might be a nice change of pace for you to have a night out after the stress of the past few weeks. To be honest, you'd also be do-ing me a favor." May as well play his trump card up-front—and set the parameters for their evening in case she thought he had any personal interest in her.

"How so?"

"Frank has a habit of trying to fix me up, and nothing I've done has convinced him I'm not interested in dating. I usually turn down his invitations, but I figured if I came to one of his parties with a date he might decide I could take care of my own social life and lay off."

A few beats ticked by.

"Um…I'm not in the habit of socializing. I try to spend all my free time with Sarah. And I'd have to find someone to watch her."

"My mom said she'd be happy to do that."

Several more silent seconds passed.

"Are you certain? I don't want to impose on her."

"Yes. I checked with her before I called you." Which had been less awkward than expected. Rather than the third degree he'd braced for, Mom had simply said, "No problem." Weird— but he'd take it.

"I, uh, don't generally stay out late. I like to have Sarah in bed by eight."

"We can make it an early night."

"In that case, I guess…I suppose I could go, Doctor. If it will help you out." She didn't sound any too certain about accepting.

"It will—if we switch to first names and ditch the titles. Otherwise, I think my partner will smell a rat." He put a slight tease into his inflection.

"I see your point." There was a touch of humor in her voice now too.

Once they agreed on a time and said their goodbyes, Eric ended the call, set his phone on the charger, and released a long breath as an odd combination of emotions swept over him. Relief. Anticipation. Uncertainty. Guilt.

Guilt?

He frowned.

Why should he feel guilty? This wasn't a real date. It was an opportunity to put a damper on Frank's matchmaking efforts and give Kate a much-needed break from the stress that was ingrained in her life. A few carefree hours would be good for her.

But if that was true…if he was thinking primarily of *her*…why was *he* looking forward to the barbecue with such eager anticipation?

3

Kate glanced in the mirror behind her bedroom door and adjusted the strap on her sundress, another wave of doubt crashing over her.

This was crazy.

She should have turned down Dr. Carlson's—Eric's—invitation.

But by positioning it as a favor to get him off the hook with his matchmaking partner, he'd made it hard to say no. Plus, both he and his mother had been clear that he wasn't interested in dating. On top of all that, she owed him after he'd come to her rescue with her day-care dilemma.

So there was no reason to feel uneasy. This wasn't a date.

Even if it felt like one.

Which explained the little niggle of guilt pricking her conscience.

Because despite the innocent setup, going with Eric to this event seemed somehow disloyal to Jack.

But it was too late to back out now.

Taking a steadying breath, she picked up her purse, left her bedroom, and joined Sarah in the living room.

Her daughter smiled at her from the couch where she was perched. "You look pretty, Mommy."

"Thanks, honey."

"I wish I could go to the party."

"Me too. But it's for grown-ups. And you'll have fun with Aunt Anna." The doorbell rang, and Kate gave Sarah a quick hug. "That's Dr. Eric. Run and get your sweater."

As Sarah scampered toward her bedroom, Kate smoothed a hand down her dress. Willed her erratic pulse to behave as she walked toward the tiny foyer in her apartment.

But it went rogue again the instant she opened the door.

The Eric who'd shown up tonight looked nothing like the doctor in the white coat, a stethoscope around his neck, who she'd encountered in the clinical setting of his office.

Instead, her pseudo date for the evening was dressed in khakis and a cobalt blue golf shirt that hugged his broad chest and matched his eyes—and he exuded a raw virility that activated her long-dormant hormones.

She clutched the edge of the door tighter. "Hi." Her greeting came out in a croak.

"Hi back." His eyes were warm, with a hint of some emotion she couldn't quite identify. "Pretty dress." He gave her outfit a quick once-over.

"Thanks." She cleared her throat, resisting the urge to tug up the modest bodice or fiddle with the spaghetti straps.

"Hi, Dr. Eric." Sarah burst into the foyer, dragging her sweater by one sleeve. "Are you coming in?"

"If your mommy invites me." One side of his mouth rose.

Warmth flooded Kate's cheeks, and she pulled the door wide. "Sorry. Please, come in."

He entered, then dropped down beside her daughter. "Are you still having those tummy aches?"

"No. They're all gone. You must be a good doctor."

His mouth flexed. "I think Dr. Anna can take the credit for your cure."

Sarah cocked her head. "Is Aunt Anna a doctor too?"

"In some ways. She always used to make me feel better after I fell off my bike and scraped my knees."

"She makes me feel good too. We're going to bake cookies tonight and watch *Mary Poppins.*"

"That sounds like fun."

"Maybe you can watch a movie with me and Mommy sometime. We make popcorn and sit on the couch. There'd be room for you."

"Um...shouldn't we be leaving?" Kate stepped in, cheeks heating up again. "I promised Sarah I wouldn't be gone too long, and it's getting late." Best remind him of their agreement to make this an early evening.

He rose. "Whenever you're ready."

As they started toward the door, Kate paused when her phone rang from inside her purse. "Do you mind if I take this? I've been waiting for a call from the mother of a student who has some health issues and had to miss the opening of school. I'm trying to help her keep him up to speed on his studies."

"No worries. I'm sure Sarah will entertain me." He smiled at her daughter.

"I'll be back in a minute."

"Don't hurry. We'll get to the party when we get there."

As Eric strolled into the living room, Sarah chattering at his side, Kate escaped to the bedroom and checked the screen of her phone.

It was the student's mother.

But even if it hadn't been, she needed a couple of minutes to rein in her pulse and restore some semblance of rhythm to her lungs.

She also needed to give herself a stern talking to.

No matter Eric's effect on her metabolism, this was *not* a date. She was simply having the reaction any normal woman would to a handsome man. There was nothing personal in it.

That was her story, and she was sticking to it.

* * *

"We can sit over there." Sarah pointed to the sofa and took his hand, towing him that direction.

Eric followed without protest, using the opportunity to survey Kate's modest apartment.

In addition to the small living room, there was a tiny kitchenette with a counter that served as a dining table. Judging by the three doors opening off the short hallway they passed, there must be two bedrooms and a bath.

He furrowed his brow.

The unit was barely large enough for two people, let alone three. How had they managed in such a confined space when Kate's mother was alive?

But apparently there'd been no choice. From what his mom had gleaned, Kate's finances were tight, and this cramped, older apartment was evidence that funds were in short supply.

Yet she'd made it a home, adding warm touches that gave the space a comfortable, inviting feel. One of Sarah's drawings had been framed and hung on the wall. A cross-stitched pillow rested on the couch. Green plants flourished in a wicker stand by the window. And several family photos were prominently displayed.

As Sarah pulled him down beside her on the couch and launched into a story about a craft project she and his mom had done, he studied the wedding photo on the side table.

In it, a slightly younger Kate and Jack looked blissfully happy, their mutual love and devotion clear in their expressions, their eyes filled with dreams about the life they were going to share together and the future they'd planned.

A future that never came to be.

"That's my daddy." Sarah finished her craft tale and pointed to the bride and groom shot.

He forced up the corners of his mouth. "He looks nice."

"Mommy says he was. She says he loved me very much." She touched the photo. "I don't remember him, though. He went to heaven right after I was born. Did you know my daddy?"

"No. I wish I had."

"Me too. Then you could tell me what he was like."

"I bet your mommy tells you stories about him."

Sarah gave a protracted sigh. "She does, but sometimes she cries, and it makes me sad. I wish I could—"

"I'm sorry for the delay. We can go now. You don't want to keep Aunt Anna waiting, do you, Sarah?"

As Kate spoke from the hallway Eric angled toward her, and the raw pain in her eyes was like a punch in the gut.

She'd obviously overheard at least part of their conversation.

Sarah stood and propped her hands on her hips. "We were waiting for *you,* Mommy."

As Kate's complexion reddened, Eric stepped in. "Now that everyone's ready to go, shall we?" He motioned toward the door.

Kate took his cue at once.

During the short drive, Sarah talked nonstop, and by the time they arrived at his mom's the awkward moment at the apartment had faded.

After chatting with his mother for a couple of minutes, Kate dropped to one knee beside Sarah. "Be a good girl, okay?"

"I will. We're going to have fun."

While Sarah seemed perfectly content to jump into her evening with his mom, it was obvious Kate was reluctant to say goodbye.

An impression she confirmed as they drove away. "This is the first time I've ever left her with a sitter, except for day care."

"She'll be fine. She and Mom are like two peas in a pod."

"I know. And I'm grateful they've clicked. But I still feel guilty for delegating her to someone else when I don't have to."

"You need a life too, Kate. One apart from Sarah. Adding a few adult social events to your schedule would be healthy. Balance is important."

She arched an eyebrow at him. "From what your mother has said, I'm thinking the physician may need to heal himself. It sounds like you keep your nose to the grindstone and never have a down minute."

What on earth had Mom been telling her?

"I do spend more hours than I should at work. But I also take time now and then to socialize." On rare occasions. "You don't have to feel guilty about not spending every free minute with Sarah."

She shrugged. "I like being with her. It's not a chore. Besides, building a social life takes time and work, and I don't know many people here. Jack and I lived in Cincinnati until a few months before Sarah was born, and when we first moved to St. Louis we were too busy fixing up our house to socialize. After the accident, I had no time to make friends. I was with Jack every minute I could spare. Since he died, I haven't had the interest or the energy to meet people. Sarah is all I need."

"Have you ever thought *she* might need more?"

Out of the corner of his eye, he saw her stiffen. "Like what?"

A caution sign began to flash in his mind

"Friends her own age." He kept his tone conversational and nonjudgmental. "Is she involved in any activities with other children?"

"There aren't many children in our apartment complex. And there's nowhere for her to play unless I take her to the park down the street." Her tone grew defensive. "We get along, Eric. It's not ideal, but then, nothing is."

Time to back off.

"You're right. And your social life is none of my business. But I appreciate your willingness to help me out tonight with mine. You'll like Frank and Mary. And maybe we'll both have some fun."

* * *

Fun.

As Eric tooled through town toward their destination, that word kept strobing through Kate's mind.

It seemed like such a foreign, distant concept.

When had she last indulged in pure, carefree fun with other adults?

Too long ago to remember.

And tonight wasn't likely to change that pattern.

Yet two hours later, she had to admit she was having fun.

Pinpointing the exact moment when she began to chill out and enjoy herself was impossible. It may have been when Frank told a hilarious story about how he and his wife met after Mary ran into his car. Or maybe it was when she got coaxed into a game of lawn darts, and much to everyone's surprise—including her own—trounced one challenger after another.

All she knew was that suddenly she found herself laughing—and relaxing.

And it felt good. So good.

As she won her fourth round of lawn darts, Frank held up his hands in defeat. "That's it. I give up. I'm not a glutton for punishment. I duly dub Kate the Queen of Lawn Darts. And now I think it's time to move on to something more important. Let's eat."

Mary gave him a good-natured poke in the ribs. "Is that all you ever think about? Food?"

He glanced down at her five-months-pregnant girth and grinned. "Obviously not."

She blushed and rolled her eyes. "I'm not going to touch that one with a ten-foot pole. Let's eat."

"Isn't that what I just said?" Frank stole a quick kiss.

As Kate watched their affectionate interplay, a sudden wave of melancholy dimmed her upbeat mood.

She and Jack had once shared that kind of closeness, where a look spoke volumes and a simple touch could unite two hearts.

But for her, those golden days were gone forever.

"Did I hear someone say food?" Eric came up behind her.

Mary planted her fists on her hips. "You men are all alike."

"I certainly hope so." Frank grinned and gave her a shoulder nudge. "Come on, we need to lead off or no one will eat." He took her hand and propelled her toward the buffet table.

As the two of them moved off, Eric turned to her and nodded toward the food line. "Shall we?"

"Sounds good." Doing her best to banish her sudden dejection, she pasted on a smile she hoped didn't look as artificial as it felt.

He followed her over to the serving table and picked up two

plates. Handed her one, then cocked his head as he studied her. "Everything okay?"

So much for trying to keep up a front.

Obviously not much got past this man.

She shrugged and forced up her stiff lips again. "I was just remembering that old cliché about how you never really appreciate something until it's gone." She looked over at Frank and Mary, who were holding hands as they carried their plates to a table. "They're a nice couple."

"Yes, they are. It renews your faith in romance to see two people whose love is deep and true."

They filled their plates in silence, and when they reached the end of the line he paused. Scanned the yard. Pointed toward a secluded table under a rose arbor. "What do you think about that spot?"

Kate glanced back toward the group. "Shouldn't we mingle?"

"We've been doing that all night. Frank and Mary won't take offense if we keep to ourselves for a little while. Yea or nay?" He nodded toward the arbor again.

Kate gave the old-fashioned garden setting a scan.

It was lovely.

But perhaps also a bit too secluded and romantic. After all, this wasn't a date.

Truth be told, though, it would be nice to have a quiet dinner in a spot like that, with adult conversation amid the scent of roses...even if a faint hint of danger seemed to be wafting through the air around them.

Yet what possible harm could come from a thirty-minute meal with her daughter's doctor?

* * *

He shouldn't have suggested such a secluded niche for dinner.

But when the joy had faded from Kate's face a few moments ago as she'd watched Frank and Mary, Eric hadn't been able to resist the impulse to get her away from a situation that was stirring up melancholy memories.

A romantic spot in a rose arbor, however, may not have been the best choice. It could give her wrong ideas.

It might be smart to regroup.

"We could also sit over—"

"That looks like a good—"

They both stopped speaking as their words overlapped.

Before he could backtrack on his suggestion, Kate's lips flexed. "Sorry. I was going to say that looks like a good spot. I love roses."

Too late to change course now.

"Then let's grab that table before someone beats us to it."

He let her lead the way, and once they were seated she sent him an apologetic glance. "I didn't mean to put a damper on your fun with my comment a minute ago. Watching Frank and Mary just reminded me of happier times." She poked at her coleslaw with the tines of her fork. "My husband and I were very much in love. Like them."

"I know."

Her eyebrows arched. "How?"

He shifted in his seat. "I could feel the love radiating from you the night of the accident. To be honest, I envied what the two of you had." A bee took a liking to his brisket, and he waved it away as the admission spilled from his mouth.

"I take it your marriage wasn't…memorable."

At her tentative comment, he swallowed past the resentment and regret that always left a sour taste in his mouth. "Oh, it was memorable. For all the wrong reasons."

"I'm sorry." The empathy in her eyes went straight to his heart. "I don't want to pry, but...well, if it would help to talk about it, I've been told I'm a good listener."

Silence fell between them as the scent of roses perfumed the air, tempering his bitterness just as Kate's compassion did.

Strange.

While he didn't often talk about that painful period in his life, for whatever reason the urge to share some of his story with this woman who'd loved and lost and harbored her own pain was too strong to resist.

"If I've overstepped, I apolo—"

"No." He held up his hand before she could retract her offer. "It's just that I don't share much about my marriage in general. And I don't want to ruin your evening with an unhappy story."

"I get the part about keeping private matters private. I've only talked to my mom and sister about everything I went through with Jack. But those venting sessions saved me." Her lips twisted. "And trust me, I'm used to unhappy stories. It won't spoil my evening. But I won't be offended if you'd rather focus on more pleasant topics."

That would be safer, no question about it.

But maybe giving voice to some of the hurt bottled inside would be healthy.

Why not test the waters? See how receptive she was?

He forced himself to take a bite of potato salad he didn't really want. Chewed. Swallowed.

After washing it down with a long swallow of tea, he resettled his cup on the table and took the plunge. "I can give you the highlights—or lowlights, depending on your perspective—if you're certain you want to hear them."

"I am."

Fisting his free hand in his lap, he inhaled another lungful of the perfumed air. "Cindy and I met when I was in medical school. She was blond and beautiful, carefree and fun, always ready for the next adventure. I was the serious, studious type, and it was exciting to be with her. I never knew what she'd do next. She added a whole new dimension to my quiet life. As different as we were, something clicked between us and I proposed a year after we met. We got married a few months later."

"So it wasn't a whirlwind courtship."

"No. I wish I could blame our problems on impulsiveness. But I thought I knew her well. That's why I was shocked when everything started to go downhill. She didn't like my choice of specialty, and she began to resent the intrusion of my career on our personal lives. The differences between us that we once found appealing gradually became irritating and hurtful. In the end, we were barely speaking."

Compassion softened her features. "It must have been hard living in that kind of environment."

"It was. For both of us." A familiar heaviness settled in his chest. "Cindy was right about my career. It sucks up a huge amount of my time. And as our marriage disintegrated, I spent even more hours in the office and at the hospital, which only made matters worse."

"Did you try counseling?"

"I suggested it. Cindy wasn't interested. And counseling wouldn't have changed my specialty."

"Why was that a problem?"

He scrubbed at a stain of barbecue sauce on the tablecloth

with the tip of his finger. "Cindy expected me to be a surgeon, which she considered a more prestigious discipline. When we got married, I was still in medical school, and surgery was where I thought I'd end up. But eventually I realized I didn't enjoy practicing medicine in that sterile environment. I wanted to interact with people. And I love kids. Pediatrics was a natural fit for me."

Her lips curved up. "I can vouch for that after watching you with Sarah. You have a gift with the younger set."

While her words warmed him, they didn't take away the lingering sting of his wife's barbs. "Cindy didn't see it that way. She was disappointed in my choice—and in me. Over time, our relationship fell apart because of that and…other issues." Enough said on that topic.

Kate reached out. Touched the fingers of the hand he'd clenched around his cup, the gentleness in her eyes a balm to his soul. "I'm sorry, Eric. The death of a spouse who's the center of your world is shattering, but the death of a happily-ever-after dream would be devastating in a different way. And equally heartrending, I imagine."

She understood.

Without him having to explain the emotions deep in his heart or the bone-deep disillusionment that had cast a shadow over his life for years, she got it.

Filling his lungs, Eric swallowed past the lump in his throat and dropped his gaze to her slender fingers lightly resting on his, their warmth seeping straight to his core.

Not once during his entire relationship with Cindy had she touched him in quite this way, with such heartfelt empathy and simple human caring.

Another tragedy in their marriage.

Because these kinds of simple touches and connections were

the bedrock of any good relationship.

"Yes. It is." His voice rasped, and he paused. Took a moment to regain his composure. "I didn't go into marriage with rose-colored glasses. I knew issues would come up that we'd have to work through, and I thought we were both committed to sticking together no matter what. That was another thing I misread about Cindy. But I still believe marriage is forever, even though she remarried and moved to Denver a few months after the divorce became final."

Kate withdrew her hand, and he missed the warmth of her touch at once. "I admire your commitment to your vows."

He managed to prop up one corner of his mouth as he cut a bite of meat. "Most people think I'm too old school. Including my mother, who's about as conservative as you can get. But that's the way I'm wired."

Brow bunching, Kate returned to her dinner too. "It has to be lonely, though."

"Sometimes." Most of the time, in truth.

"May I ask how you cope with that? Because it's a problem for me too."

"Some days are a struggle, but family and faith help. My parents have always been a great support system, and even though Dad is gone now, Mom's still a wonderful nurturer." When she wasn't trying to convince him to rejoin the dating scene. "I'm also active in my church, and I've had quite a few long talks with my pastor."

"I have the family part, anyway. Thanks to my sister."

He frowned at the disconnect. "I must have misunderstood a comment Mom made. I thought she said Sarah had mentioned going to church."

Kate's lips contorted into a rueful twist. "You didn't misunderstand. My mother used to take her. I should pick up the slack, but when Jack died I stopped going to church. After months of fruitless pleading and begging and bargaining with God to save him, I decided that if God wasn't listening, why bother praying? I do feel guilty about not taking Sarah to church, but I'm still not ready to go back."

A theological discussion wasn't on his agenda for tonight, nor did he feel equipped to talk someone back from the ledge of apostasy, but he could at least help on one score.

"I can think of a simple fix for your guilt about Sarah. Mom and I would be happy to take her with us to church on Sunday."

Kate blinked, then shook her head. "I couldn't ask you to do that. You've both helped me out too much already. It wouldn't be right."

"You didn't ask. I offered. And think about it as a favor for Sarah rather than for you."

She broke off a bite of biscuit as she considered him. "Were you by chance on the debate team in high school or college?"

"No way." He gave her a look of mock horror. "I was on the shy side in my younger days. Still am to some degree when I'm not in doctor mode."

Her expression grew skeptical. "That's hard to believe. You project confidence and self-assurance and authority."

"A positive byproduct of medical training. But those traits are more evident in my professional life than in my personal life." He took a swig of iced tea.

"I'll have to take your word for that. As for church, I can't argue with your rationale. And I know my mom would be disappointed if I let Sarah's faith lapse along with my own. You're certain you don't mind?"

"Not in the least. We can start tomorrow."

They worked out a pick-up time, since he'd be passing close to her house on the way to his mother's.

"Thank you again for offering to do this." She speared a stray strawberry and popped it in her mouth. "Maybe Sarah will make a few new friends there if they have any children's programs."

"They do, and I expect she will. I'll have Mom bring a schedule home for you so you can look over the youth offerings." He set his knife on the side of his plate. "You'd be welcome to join us for services anytime."

As the invitation spilled out of his mouth, he frowned.

Where had *that* come from?

If he wanted to keep his distance, this could be a huge tactical mistake.

Fortunately, Frank jogged over before she could respond. "The conversation looks way too serious over here. Time to liven things up a little. Kate, I challenge you to one more round of lawn darts. I feel renewed after that meal." He patted his stomach.

She smiled, glanced at her watch, and set her fork on her plate, next to the remnants of her meal. "I should get home."

"Eric, convince her."

He finished his last bite, wiped his lips on a paper napkin, and smiled at her. "Let me just say he'll be a bear at work if he doesn't get a chance to redeem himself."

Mouth bowing, Kate capitulated. "Okay. One more round."

Fifteen minutes later, after she once again gave their host a sound beating, she and Eric said their goodbyes and strolled toward his car.

"He'll never live this down, you know." Eric took her arm as they traversed an uneven section of lawn.

Did her breath hitch—or was that his imagination?

"It was only a game of lawn darts. How many people will

remember the outcome a week from now?"

Not his imagination.

She sounded a bit winded.

And much to his chagrin, he could relate.

Being close to Kate, with her sweet, fresh scent tickling his nose reminded him of all he'd been missing for so many years—and awakened in him a yearning for things he could never have again.

And that was bad.

He dropped her arm as soon as they were back on level ground and called up his most jocular tone. It was best to keep things light and friendly. Nothing more. "*I'll* remember."

"Eric!" She looked over at him in the fading light. "You aren't going to use this against him, are you?"

"Of course I am. What are friends for?" He opened her door and stepped back to let her slide inside.

She paused by the seat, humor glinting in her irises. "He's going to be sorry I came with you tonight."

"Maybe. But I'm not."

At his husky admission, she froze.

Blast.

That had slipped out before he could stop it.

Time for damage control.

"He's held the lawn dart champion title for too long. It's time for someone else to take the podium." He motioned her into the car. "Let's go get Sarah."

She slid onto the seat, and he closed the door. Circled the car in slow motion, willing his racing pulse to slow, his muddled brain to unclog, and his unruly tongue to behave.

Implying to Kate that he was interested in her in any sort of romantic sense would be a huge mistake. It was obvious she still loved her husband, and he wasn't in the market for a new relationship.

So going forward, he should keep his distance.

Except for picking Sarah up on Sundays.

But he didn't have to linger during the hand-off.

And he wouldn't.

No matter how tempted he might be.

4

She needed to get a handle on her feelings.

As Kate paced in her tiny foyer while she waited for Eric to pick up Sarah for church, she tried to calm her roiling emotions.

A task she'd worked on with negligible success throughout her restless night after the barbecue.

They should never have shared dinner under that rose arbor. That had been mistake number one.

Mistake number two had been encouraging Eric to tell her about his marriage. How could any caring person's heart not go out to a man who'd been trapped in a loveless union and whose dreams of a lifetime partnership had crashed and burned?

The third mistake had been agreeing to let him take Sarah to church with him and his mom. While that may have been in her daughter's best interest, it had done nothing to restore her own equilibrium.

Because now she'd have to see Eric every week—and try to figure out how to deal with the guilt-producing buzz of adrenaline that pulsed through her nerve endings whenever she was in his presence.

Nor did it help that his insightful eyes seemed to see straight into her soul—and perhaps discern that she liked him too much.

But while she was no longer bound by the till-death-do-us-part vow she'd made to Jack, in every way that mattered she still felt married to her husband.

So being attracted to Eric felt wrong, even if nothing could ever come of it, given Eric's commitment to his own marriage vows. Because it felt like a betrayal of Jack.

At the sudden ring of the bell, she jerked and swung toward the door, hand flying to her chest.

"I'll answer it, Mommy." Sarah dashed past her and twisted the knob.

With Eric's attention distracted by his young greeter, Kate had a moment to take a quick inventory once the door swung open.

And attraction reared its unsettling head again.

His classic Nordic good looks were on full display today, and though it sounded fanciful, in a different age he could have stood at the helm of a questing ship. Yet his gentle manner and kindheartedness were at odds with the fierce Viking images of old. It seemed he'd inherited the best of both worlds—the athletic virility of his ancestors and the sensibilities of a modern male. It was a stunning—and appealing—combination.

Today, in a crisp, open-necked Oxford shirt, sport coat, and gray slacks that emphasized his lean, muscular frame, he could have stepped from the pages of *GQ*.

As her heart flip-flopped, he straightened up from greeting Sarah and looked over to her with a quiet smile. "Good morning."

"Morning. Sarah's ready to go." She crossed to her daughter and adjusted the ribbon in her hair.

Anna peeked around her son, a plastic-wrapped plate in hand. "Good morning, my dear. I made a batch of cinnamon rolls yesterday and thought you and Sarah might like a few." She held out the offering.

"You're going to spoil us. But thank you." She took the plate. "They look delicious."

"I hope you enjoy them. I also wanted to invite you and Sarah to join Eric and me for breakfast. We go out every Sunday after the service. It wouldn't be any bother to swing back by here and pick you up."

Kate peeked at Eric.

He seemed as taken aback by his mother's suggestion as she was.

"Can we, Mommy?" Sarah's eyes were sparkling. "I could get pancakes." She swiveled toward the mother/son duo. "I like pancakes a whole bunch."

"Eric does too." Anna smiled at her. "Don't you, Eric?" She nudged him with her elbow.

The twin furrows scoring his brow didn't ease. "Yes."

He was clearly not in favor of a breakfast party, despite their pleasant evening at the barbecue.

Or perhaps because of it.

Maybe he was also battling the subtle stirrings of attraction that plagued *her*.

Kate called up a smile. "I appreciate the offer, Anna, but I have to work on lesson plans."

"Well, perhaps another time. It's important to have social interaction, you know. It isn't good to work all the time—as I'm forever telling my son." She sent Eric a reproving glance.

"I don't work *all* the time."

"I suppose that's a slight exaggeration. After all, you did make a rare exception and go to that barbecue last night with Kate. Say…" Her face lit up a bit too brightly, as if whatever she was about to say wasn't quite as impromptu as she was trying to suggest. "Why don't you take her to that fancy shindig you're going to next Saturday? You haven't filled your plus-one slot, and it would give her a chance to dress up, go out on the town, and have an elegant dinner."

Kate stared at her.

So did Eric.

It was hard to tell who was more dumbfounded.

But Eric recovered faster than she did. "Those events are pretty boring, Mom. And it's not fair to put Kate on the spot." He angled toward her. "I serve on the board of a health-related organization, and the dinner Mom is referring to is an annual fundraiser for the group."

"That's one of the many boards he's on." Anna rolled her eyes. "It's harder for you to say no to a good cause than for a gopher to stop digging holes. I know you don't like these black-tie events, but they might be more pleasant if you took someone. And I bet Kate would enjoy an evening like that."

"Are you guys talking about another party?" Sarah joined the conversation. "Like the one Mommy and Dr. Eric went to last night?"

"Yes, only much fancier." Anna smiled down at her.

"I think you should go, Mommy. Aunt Anna and I could make cookies again and watch another movie. And you told me you had a lot of fun. I heard you singing in the kitchen this morning."

Kate cringed.

Could the floor please open up and swallow her right now?

"Out of the mouths of babes…" Anna beamed at Sarah.

Willing the heat on her cheeks to subside, Kate risked another stealthy glance at Eric.

Her barbecue partner was giving his mother a narrow-eyed look. But when his gaze swung toward her, he telegraphed a silent apology before he spoke. "I'll discuss it with Kate later. Right now we need to get to church."

Without further ado, he ushered the other two females toward the door.

But on the threshold he turned back to her and spoke in a low voice as Anna continued toward the car, Sarah's hand clasped in hers. "Sorry about that. Mom's on a mission to beef up my social life, just like my partner is."

She conjured up a smile. "No worries. She could give Yente a run for her money—if you've seen *Fiddler on the Roof*."

"I have—and I agree. Mom must have inherited a match-maker gene from someone in our family tree." He took a step back. "I'll have Sarah home safe and sound in less than two hours. No need to worry about her."

"I won't. I know she's in good hands."

She waited by the window while he returned to his car, watching as they pulled away. Then she wandered into the living room and sank onto the couch.

That had been beyond awkward.

Of course Anna had meant well. She cared about Eric's well-being, wanted to see him happy. And she wanted those grandchildren she'd mentioned.

But he was old enough to plan his own social life. If he wanted to ask someone out, he would.

However…what if he *had* invited her to that fancy dinner?

Her stomach fluttered, and she pressed a hand against it. Drew a shaky breath as she reached for the wedding photo beside her and traced the contours of Jack's dear, familiar face with a trembling finger.

In the almost eleven years since they'd been joined as man and wife, her love for him hadn't diminished one iota.

But other things had.

Certain images and sensory memories were slipping away, despite her desperate efforts to hold on to them. The exaggerated, comical dismay on his face whenever she served carrots at dinner.

The deep timbre of his voice during their intimate moments. The evening bristle on his jaw beneath her fingertips. The distinctive, woodsy scent of his aftershave. The way he always tilted his head as he cut the grass.

All of those were fading, like an old photograph in which only vague outlines remained of images that had once been sharp and clear and vibrant.

Soon she would only be able to remember the *fact* that those things had once been special, not the unique qualities that made them so.

Pressure built in her throat, and she hugged the wedding photo tight against her chest. Closed her eyes.

The truth was, she was losing Jack, bit by bit, day by day, and there was nothing she could do to stop the sense of distance and the ebbing of memories that had accelerated in the past few months. Nor could she banish the sick, hollow, helpless feeling that accompanied that sense of loss.

Yet that feeling did abate in the presence of Eric Carlson. The very man who'd saved her husband's life on that icy night, and who was now awakening needs that had lain dormant for five long years. Stirring up yearnings she'd never expected to feel again.

How was she supposed to deal with that?

No answer came to mind—but a voice of reason and understanding was only a phone call away. And she needed to hear it. Bad.

After replacing the photo on the side table, she dug out her phone and tapped in her sister's number.

Amy answered on the second ring. "Kate? What's wrong?" There was a hint of panic in her voice.

"Nothing. Why?"

"You never call this early on Sunday morning."

That was true. Because Amy and her family were always at church.

Man, her brain must be really muddled.

Except...why was Amy home today?

"I think I should ask *you* that question. Why aren't you at church?"

"Cal pulled a midnight shift at the park last night and is sleeping in. We're going to the second service. So why the out-of-pattern call? The last time this happened you were lamenting a two-grand repair bill on your car."

"Which you graciously helped me pay until I could get my finances in order. But I'm not calling about money today."

"You know we'll help if you ever have cash flow problems, though, right? Cal and I get that you're a single working mother with huge medical debts."

"And you have three kids, are married to a man who makes his living dressed like Smokey the Bear, live in a log cabin, and make quilts to keep the wolf from the door."

Amy snorted a laugh. "A gross oversimplification."

True, but it had lightened the atmosphere. "I know. And I also know you love every minute of your life."

A contented sigh came over the line. "Yeah, I do. But there are days I wish we were rich. Then we could do more to help you."

"You do the most important thing. You're there for me when I need a friendly and encouraging ear. That's worth more than gold."

"Still, gold comes in handy sometimes. How are you doing with the medical bills?"

"Getting there. I pay off a little every month. I figure at this rate I'll be free and clear about the time I'm ready to retire." She tried for a light tone but couldn't quite pull it off.

"I'm sorry you have to deal with that burden, Kate. I know Jack would be too." A few beats ticked by, and when she continued her voice was more subdued. "Maybe I shouldn't say this, but I think if he'd known how things were going to turn out he would have told the good Samaritan who stopped that night to keep driving."

So did she, in the deepest corner of her heart.

But that didn't diminish the heroic attempt Eric had made that icy night to save his life.

"Actually, that good Samaritan is one of the reasons I called today. You'll never believe this coincidence, but he's Sarah's new pediatrician."

"Seriously? What a weird fluke. Did he recognize you?"

"Yes. And the story gets stranger. His mother is now watching Sarah while I teach."

The scraping sound of a chair being pulled across the floor came over the line. "I have to sit down to take all this in. How in the world did you arrange that?"

"I didn't. He did." Kate gave Amy the short version, ending with Eric's offer to take Sarah to church each Sunday.

"Man, did you luck out. My pediatrician is great, but I doubt she'd ever take such a personal interest in my kids." A beat ticked by. "Is this guy, by any chance, single?"

Leave it to Amy to pick up the nuances and drill straight to the heart of the matter. Must come from her years of investigative reporting.

"Divorced."

"So he's available."

"Not according to him or his mother." She gave Amy the

topline. "He did ask me to go with him to his partner's barbecue last night, but it wasn't a real date. He said his partner has been trying to beef up his social life, and he wanted to convince him he didn't need any help with that."

"Uh-huh." Amy didn't sound convinced. "Did you have fun?"

She rose. Began to pace. "It was nice to have an evening out with adults."

"That's a hedge. So let me try a different tack. If he asked you out again, would you go?"

"He won't. He had a chance to do that this morning, and he blew it off." She told Amy about his mother's suggestion for the black-tie dinner.

"Hmm. I imagine that took him by surprise. But what if he decides to follow through after he thinks it over? Hypothetically speaking."

A kaleidoscope of butterflies took off in her stomach. "He won't."

"What if he does?"

"I should say no."

"Why? Don't you like him?"

That wasn't the problem.

The problem was she liked him too much.

"He's a very nice man. But he's not in the market for a relationship, and neither am I."

"I understand where he's coming from based on what you said, even if his attitude is unusual in this day and age. But why would *you* write off a new relationship?"

She stopped by the window. Massaged her temples as she watched a male and female cardinal snuggle side by side on the branch of an oak tree. "I still love Jack, Amy."

"Of course you do. You always will. You two had an amazing marriage. But you're a young, vibrant woman, and you've been living in an emotional cave for too long. There's nothing wrong with moving on after all this time."

"Except I still feel married. Getting involved in a romance with someone else would seem disloyal."

A few beats ticked by. "Look, I'll say this straight out, okay? I know you loved Jack. And he was a great guy. We *all* loved him, and we all still miss him. We always will. When I think of life without Cal…well, it makes me understand in a very small way the pain and grief you've had to deal with. But Jack wouldn't want you to go through the rest of your life without ever really living again, Kate. And part of living is loving."

Her throat constricted. "I have Sarah."

"I'm not talking about that type of love. You're the kind of woman who was meant to be in a loving, committed relationship. That's not to say you're not strong or capable or independent. You're all of those things, and you've proved it over and over again these past five years. But Jack wouldn't want you to close yourself off to life—and love—because of a misplaced sense of obligation or guilt. He'd want you to start making some memories instead of living alone with the old ones, happy as they are."

As the male cardinal nuzzled the female, Kate swiped at her lashes.

As usual, Amy had nailed the pertinent facts of the situation with her razor-sharp insight. People didn't always like what her sister said, but they could rarely deny the truth of her conclusions.

"I'm not disputing anything you've said. But it's…it's hard to let go." Her voice choked.

"I know." Empathy softened Amy's words. "But you're going to have to do that before you can get on with your life."

"I may have to do that whether I want to or not. Jack's kind of…he's slipping away anyway."

"Oh, Kate." Her sister's voice scraped. "I wish I were there right now to give you a hug."

"Me too. I don't want to lose what I have left of Jack, and I'm afraid if I start to move on the memories will fade even faster."

"Being scared is normal whenever we think about making a big change in our life. But remember the old saying about ships. They may be safe in the harbor, but that's not what they're built for. I think it's time for you to set sail, Kate. If not with Eric, at least open the door to someone else."

Kate leaned a shoulder against the window frame as the two cardinals took flight, stretching their wings to soar toward a new destination. "How come you always know the right thing to say?"

A snort came over the line. "My kids wouldn't agree with that."

"They will when they get older." Cal called out in the background, and Kate turned away from the window. "I know you have to get ready for church. Thanks for being my sounding board, and give everyone a hug for me."

"Will do. I'll call you next week. Love you, Sis."

"Love you back."

Once they ended the call, Kate wandered back to the side table by the couch. Rested her fingers on top of the frame as Jack smiled back at her, all the joy of their wedding day reflected in his glowing face, his eyes filled with hopes and dreams for their tomorrows.

But now all that was left was their yesterdays.

Except she still had a lot of tomorrows ahead of her, barring another tragedy like the one that had taken Jack's life.

And Amy was right.

With his zest for life and his belief in living every day to the fullest, he wouldn't want her to live the rest of her life lonely and sad. Nor would he want her to lock away all the love in her heart that was meant for sharing.

Intellectually, she could accept that.

Emotionally, she wasn't there yet.

But perhaps one of these days, if the right person came along, she'd find the courage to leave the past behind and embrace a new tomorrow.

* * *

"So you've been holding out on your old pal all this time."

Eric glanced up from his laptop to find Frank lounging against the door frame of his office, arms folded, one ankle crossed over the other, his accusatory tone tempered by the twinkle in his eyes.

"What's that supposed to mean?" As if he didn't know. He'd been waiting all day for his partner to give him the third degree about Kate. If they hadn't been so slammed with day-after-a-holiday crises, Frank would no doubt have waylaid him far earlier.

"You know very well what I mean. Here I think you're a miserable, lonely, driven man in desperate need of female companionship, and then you show up with a hottie like Kate. Boy, you had me fooled. Where have you been hiding her all this time?"

"I haven't been hiding her anywhere. And I'm not sure she'd appreciate the term hottie. Why don't we just refer to her as the Queen of Lawn Darts?"

Frank grimaced. "Ouch! You would have to bring that up. I

just had an off night. So…" He ambled over and propped a hip on the edge of the desk. "Tell me everything. Where did you meet this goddess? And how serious are you two?"

"We're friends. Nothing more at this point." Or ever.

"Uh-huh."

"I mean it."

"You expect me to buy that after the way you were looking at her all night?"

Eric frowned. "What do you mean?"

"Come on, man. You hung on her every word. You made it a point to keep tabs on her whenever you were apart—which wasn't often. And you have the look."

"What look?"

"Smitten. Enamored. Head over heels. Is that descriptive enough?"

Eric waved him off. "You're crazy."

"Nope. I know what I saw. I had that look once myself. Still do sometimes, in fact."

"Well, with all due respect to your powers of perception, you're off base this time, pal."

Frank grinned and stood. "Good try, but no sale. However, I get the message—butt out. I can read a *No Trespassing* sign when I see one." He ambled to the door and disappeared into the hall, but a moment later he stuck his head back inside. "But I don't pay attention to signs. I'll wear you down eventually. In the meantime, your secret's safe with me."

As Frank disappeared again, Eric let out a slow breath.

While his partner might be a bit outspoken and on the boisterous side, his powers of perception were keen. He could nail a person's personality within five minutes of meeting them, and he was even more intuitive with friends and associates. Sometimes it was almost scary.

Like right now.

Eric wiped a hand down his face.

Right or wrong, he did feel more for Kate than friendship. Otherwise he wouldn't have bared his soul to her while they shared a dinner under Frank's rose arbor.

And what he felt wasn't hard to identify. It was attraction, pure and simple.

Except it wasn't simple.

Much as he might wish he could get to know her better, in his heart he still felt married. Despite the problems that had plagued his union with Cindy, he'd spoken vows before God. And he'd never had any problem sticking to them.

Until now.

He leaned back in his chair. Pinched the bridge of his nose.

Even if he was interested in pursuing Kate, however, her heart still belonged to her husband. Plus, he wasn't adept at juggling medicine and marriage, as Cindy had told him on numerous occasions.

So letting his feelings get out of hand would be a recipe for disaster.

Meaning that other than stopping by for Sarah on Sundays, he needed to—

His cell began to vibrate on his desk, and he picked it up.

Huh.

In general, his mother didn't call him during office hours unless she had an urgent issue to discuss.

Pulse accelerating, he put the phone to his ear. "Hi, Mom. What's up?"

"Are you busy?"

"Winding down for the day." With patients, anyway. There was still chart work to do.

"Kate just picked up Sarah."

He squinted at his medical school diploma on the opposite wall. "Okay." That alone shouldn't merit a call.

"She looked tired."

"Maybe she had a tough day at school. Kids can be a handful."

"I asked her about that. She said she hadn't slept very well the past couple of nights. I think she has something on her mind. Did she say anything to you at the barbecue?"

"Not about any specific worries."

"It could be a money issue, I suppose. I'm sure her husband's medical bills weigh on her mind. And being a single parent has to be challenging." A sigh came over the line. "That young woman needs some fun in her life. Did you think any more about inviting her to that dinner next weekend?"

"No."

"Why not? It would be an act of charity."

Maybe.

But it could also stir up longings best kept locked away.

A concern he had no intention of sharing with his mother.

"She likes to spend her free hours with Sarah."

Mom made a dismissive sound. "Sarah would be fine here with me. I enjoy her company. Being with her makes me feel young again."

The very goal he'd been aiming for when he'd suggested the arrangement.

But much as Mom and Sarah seemed to hit it off, they didn't need to spend Saturday nights together too.

"I'm glad to hear that, but weekend babysitting wasn't part of the deal."

A couple of beats passed.

"Why don't you want to ask her? It doesn't have to be a date, you know. You could make it clear the invitation is nothing more than a friendly gesture. No romance involved. I can't imagine why you'd choose to go to that dinner alone when you could have the company of a lovely woman like Kate."

He could.

Because if he spent another evening in her company in a pseudo-dating situation, he'd only want the real thing even more.

"It's not a good idea, Mom."

"Whyever not? Don't you think Kate would enjoy a fancy dinner?"

"I imagine she would, but—"

"Don't you think she deserves a nice evening out after all she's been through?"

"Of course. But—"

"Don't you think it's kind of selfish not to at least offer her the opportunity, since you can bring a guest? I doubt Kate's budget allows for many fast-food meals, let alone the kind of elegant meal they'll serve at that fancy do."

It was hard to counter any of her arguments.

His mother should have been a prosecuting attorney.

"I'll think about it, okay?" That's all he was going to promise.

"Don't overthink it, Eric. You know in your heart what's right. Just do it."

She ended the call soon after that, and once the line went dead he set his cell on his desk. Tapped a finger against the arm of his chair. Shook his head.

Moms could be amazingly adept at playing the guilt card.

And she was right on all counts. Kate would enjoy a fancy dinner, she did deserve a nice evening out, and it *was* selfish to deny her that opportunity just because he was running scared.

Meaning he was about to make a phone call he might very well come to regret.

* * *

There was no reason to be nervous. Having dinner with Eric in the company of a couple hundred other people was about as safe as it got for an evening out.

Nevertheless, she still should have turned him down when he'd called.

Frowning, Kate leaned closer to the mirror and adjusted her earring.

His logic had been hard to refute, however. It *would* do her good to get out more. She was becoming a hermit in her off-work hours. And he'd assured her the evening was nothing more than a social obligation to him. On top of all that, he'd admitted being guilted into asking her by his mother. How unromantic was that?

Bottom line, there was nothing personal about this nondate. Not a thing.

But if that was true, why couldn't she throw off her case of nerves?

"You look pretty, Mommy. Is that a new dress?"

At Sarah's question, Kate forced up the corners of her mouth. "No, honey. I've had this for a long time." But she'd had to forage deep into the recesses of her closet to find something suitable for a black-tie event.

"From when Daddy was here?"

A pang of grief rippled through her, but she did her best to hold on to her smile. "Yes. It's as old as you are."

"I've never seen it."

"That's because I don't go very many fancy places. And if I wore this to school, my students wouldn't recognize me, would they?"

Her daughter giggled. "I guess not. But I like it. It makes you look kind of like a movie star."

Movie star?

Ha.

The sleeveless black sheath had only made her keeper list when she'd purged her closet because it was practical. The dress could be paired with a jacket for a business look or accented with costume jewelry for a dressier effect. Tonight, a clunky hammered-gold necklace and matching earrings added a touch of glamour, and she'd arranged her hair in a more sophisticated style, but she was far from red carpet ready. Truth be told, the outfit might not even be dressy enough for a black-tie event. But it was the best she had.

If she was movie-star beautiful in her daughter's eyes, though, she'd take it.

"Thank you, honey." She leaned down and gave her a squeeze.

A moment later, her heart lurched when the doorbell rang.

"I'll get it." Sarah scampered off.

Forcing herself to take deep, slow breaths, Kate added a final touch of lipstick as she eavesdropped on the conversation in the living room.

"Hi, Dr. Eric. Hi, Aunt Anna."

"Hello there, Sarah." Eric's deep, mellow voice drifted down the hall.

"Hello, Sarah." Anna sounded chipper. "Are you ready to have fun tonight?"

"Yes!"

As the two of them exchanged a few more words, Kate quashed another pang of guilt.

It would have been easier for Anna to keep Sarah at her place overnight, as she'd offered to do since the dinner could run late. But Kate had balked. She and Sarah had never spent a night apart. Besides, what if Sarah had gotten homesick in the wee hours?

That would have been far more inconvenient than having Anna watch her here.

"Mommy is almost ready. She looks really pretty. Do you think Mommy is pretty, Dr. Eric?"

Oh, mercy.

She had to get out there now, before Sarah asked any other embarrassing questions.

"Yes, I do." Eric sounded more amused than flustered.

Lucky him.

Willing the heat on her cheeks to subside, she grabbed her purse, flipped off the light, and hurried down the hall.

"Here's Kate now." Anna gave her a bright smile. "My dear, you look lovely."

"Thanks, Anna. Hello, Eric." She flicked a glance at him.

Tried not to stare.

His black tux was a perfect complement to his blond hair, and the formal jacket sat well on his tall, muscular frame, emphasizing his broad shoulders and dignified bearing.

She might not be Hollywood glamorous, but her escort was.

"Mommy, how come your face is red?" Sarah linked her hands behind her back and tipped her head as she scrutinized her.

Anna stepped in, bless her. "Because she put on more makeup and extra blush to go with her fancy dress." She smiled at Sarah, then turned her attention to them. "You two should be on your way or you'll miss dinner. And don't hurry back. I'm deep into a mystery that will keep me entertained after Sarah goes to bed."

"I think these two are ready to get their own party started." Eric's lips quirked as his gaze connected with hers. "Ready?"

"Yes."

Yet as he stepped aside to let her pass, a faint hint of his appealing cologne tickling her nose, she acknowledged the truth.

While she was ready for an elegant evening and a gourmet meal, she most definitely was *not* ready for the tingle in her fingertips or the blender in her stomach or the sparks crackling in the air that made this feel all too much like a real date...and stirred up longings that would only cause trouble if they ever escaped from the locked box she'd placed them in the day she'd buried her husband.

5

As Eric drove away from Kate's apartment, he sent her a side-long glance.

Given her tense posture, she was as nervous as he was.

Was it because this evening felt a bit awkward—or because she'd been as blindsided as he'd been by the electrical storm back in her apartment?

No way to know for sure. It was possible his reaction had been one-sided.

But no guy with a beating heart would have been able to suppress a surge of testosterone when Kate walked out in that killer, figure-hugging dress that showed off her slender curves to perfection. Not to mention the high heels that drew attention to her spectacular legs.

At least he'd had enough presence of mind to clamp his lips together so his jaw didn't drop.

Once they were in the crowd of people at the event, it would be easier to ignore the voltage swirling through the air on his end.

However, they had to get there first.

So he needed to find a way to cut through the tension or Kate wouldn't enjoy herself tonight. Which was the whole point of this outing his mother had orchestrated.

He took a steadying breath and called up a conversational tone. "It's amazing how Mom and Sarah have hit it off, isn't it?"

"Yes. And in only two weeks." She angled a bit toward him. "What a difference from our brief day care center experience. And it seems your diagnosis of her problem was spot-on. No more tummy aches since she's been going to your mom's. This arrangement has already been such a blessing."

"For Mom too. She seems much more like her old self."

"I'm glad it's worked out for both of them. If I can't stay home with Sarah, this is the next best thing to having my mom take care of her. Being in a loving environment is so important for children, especially in their early years."

"True. At the risk of sounding prehistoric, I often think it would be better for a couple that can afford it to forego one income and give their children a full-time parent. Kids would rather have time and attention from their parents than material things."

"Jack and I felt the same. That's why I quit my job when Sarah was born." Out of the corner of his eye he saw her studying him. "I hope this comment isn't out of line, but with the way you love children I'm surprised you didn't have any. You'd make a great father."

His stomach clenched as she broached a subject he rarely discussed.

He could blow off her comment, move on to another subject, and Kate wouldn't press him.

But she already knew he'd been in a bad relationship. What was the harm of talking about this topic?

"I appreciate that. And I always assumed I'd have my own children someday. I thought Cindy was on the same page, but she kept putting off starting a family. She said we should wait for a better time—but it never came. And once our marriage started to fall apart, I didn't want to bring a child into that mess. In the end, she admitted she'd never wanted kids because they would have cramped her style. Plus, as she often reminded me, if I was too busy with my career to spend time with her, how would I ever find time to spend with children? I suppose she had a point."

"I'm not certain about that." Kate shook her head. "Most married doctors have families. I think there's a way to make almost anything work if you're committed enough. My sister is a good example of that."

Her words warmed him, even if he wasn't as optimistic as she was.

But enough about him. Time to shift the focus back to her.

"I get the feeling you and your sister are tight."

"We are." He could hear the smile in her voice as he passed a slower-moving car. "I'd love to see her more often, but she lives in Tennessee. So we have to rely on phone calls, texts, and emails to stay in touch."

"Tennessee isn't too far away, though. A day's drive or less, right? That seems doable."

"Except our schedules are hectic. Her husband, Cal, is an attorney *and* a part-time ranger in Great Smoky Mountains National Park, so his busy season is summer. They can never get away then, and I'm teaching the rest of the year. Besides, it's tough for them to travel with three small children—four-year-old twins and a six-month-old."

He gave a low whistle. "She *does* have her hands full."

"That's putting it mildly. She's also a broadcast journalist, and she hosts a bi-weekly program on a Christian cable station in Knoxville. Anyway, Sarah, Mom, and I always went down over spring break and again at Thanksgiving. But that's about it."

"Thanksgiving in the Smokies." His mouth curved up. "That sounds like a perfect getaway."

"It is. Especially at Amy's. She's become quite the earth

mother. They live in a log cabin, and she makes quilts and bakes bread and cans vegetables. I never expected that, because in her twenties she was a gung-ho career woman who liked bright lights and traveling in the fast lane and thought life ceased to exist outside the city limits."

He glanced over at her as he hung a right. "What happened?"

"Cal."

"Ah." He hiked up one side of his mouth. "True love."

"Yes. And it wasn't that she changed for him. She just discovered she'd been living a lie. That somewhere along the way she'd bought into the notion that success is only measured in dollars and prestige and power. But she was never happy, even though she had all those things. It took Cal to make her realize that."

"That's quite a story. It reaffirms your belief in happy endings."

"Yes, it does. They're a great couple." As Eric turned into the curving drive of the venue, Kate eyed the upscale hotel. "I have to admit I'm looking forward to a dinner I didn't cook—hopefully with a dessert to die for."

"I haven't seen the menu for tonight, but in general the food here is first class. We should be in for a treat."

On more than one front for him.

A delicious dessert would be fine. But he was looking even more forward to enjoying dinner in the company of a beautiful, caring, articulate woman with rock-solid values.

Unfortunately, that wasn't how it played out. Though they sat side-by-side during the meal, Kate was kept occupied by a major contributor to the organization seated to her left—and interrupting their animated conversation would have been rude.

Only when her dinner companion rose to mingle with other

guests did Eric have a few minutes alone with her. "You seem to have made a friend in Omar." He nodded toward the mild-mannered, courtly older man who was now greeting guests at a nearby table.

"He's a fascinating person." She sent the man an appreciative glance. "You'd never guess by looking at him that he did undercover work for the State Department in the Middle East in his younger years, would you?"

What?

Eric stared at her. "Seriously?"

"You didn't know?"

"No. All I knew was that he immigrated to the US as a child with his family and created a worldwide clothing empire from nothing. You learned more about his background in one dinner than I have in ten years. Speaking of having a way with people." He shook his head. "I may be able to connect with kids, but you have a knack with adults."

She shrugged off the compliment, soft color stealing across her cheeks. "I'm interested in people's stories. Everyone has one if you dig deep enough. And his is fascinating." The sparkle in her eyes was new—and uber appealing.

"So you're glad you came?"

"Yes. It's a lovely event." Her mouth curved up as she gave the fresh flowers on the tables, the crystal chandeliers, and the orchestra just beginning to tune up a sweep.

"The fundraising committee always does a first-class job. And it's a worthy cause. Abused kids need all the help they can get."

She refocused on him, her gold necklace glinting against her creamy skin in the candlelight. "Your commitment to children— on and off the job—is impressive."

He tried to focus on her face rather than the delicate curve of her neck. It wasn't easy. "Or I'm a pushover who never learned to say no."

She refused to let him downplay his charitable efforts. "Sorry. Not buying. I think you say yes because you have a generous heart."

"I appreciate the kind words, but I do have a tendency to overextend. More so since the divorce. It's gotten to the point that Frank is calling me a driven man and Mom keeps telling me to get a life."

She played with the stem of her water glass as she scrutinized him. "How do you feel about their assessment?"

"They're right. My terms on two boards are up at the end of the year and I've already decided not to renew. But I'll stay on this one. I've been involved too long to—"

"May I interrupt?"

Eric angled toward the board president, who'd stopped beside him. "Of course."

"My apologies for intruding." He sent Kate a contrite look. "But I could use your help. We need some people to kick off the dancing. I think if I get four or five of the board members out on the floor, everyone will loosen up. I'm making the rounds now. Give it a go, okay?" Without waiting for a response, he hurried off.

Eric watched him until he disappeared into the crowd, heart stammering.

Dance with Kate? Hold her close in his arms? Play with fire?

Not on his agenda for the evening.

When he shifted back to her, she gave him a rueful look. "That sounded like a command performance."

"I don't think we have to worry about losing our heads if we sit this out. Our board president doesn't have that kind of power." He put a touch of humor in his inflection.

"I suppose not." She focused on the orchestra as the bandleader moved to the front and took his position, a hint of longing in her eyes...unless he was misreading her.

He frowned.

Did *she* want to dance?

"Are you a dancer?" He kept this tone conversational.

A sweet smile curved her lips. "I used to love to dance. My dad taught me and my sister the basic ballroom moves when we were teenagers. Jack claimed he had two left feet, so I haven't danced since my wedding." She gave the floor another scan. "I'm really out of practice, so getting out on there would probably be a bad idea. What about you? Do you dance?"

"I used to. Early in our marriage Cindy dragged me to lessons. Much to my surprise, I not only enjoyed them, I became a decent dancer. But I'm out of practice too."

The band struck up "Fly Me to the Moon," and in his peripheral vision he saw Kate's toe start tapping.

"You could foxtrot to that one." The comment was out before he could stop it.

"Yes." She gave him a wary once-over, the conflict in her eyes impossible to miss.

She wanted to dance, but she was nervous about it. Just like he was.

Nevertheless, his goal tonight was to help her have a little fun. So if she wanted to dance, he should suck it up and ask her.

But he'd only be doing this for her.

Sure you would, Carlson.

He stifled the sarcastic voice in his head.

"Would you like to give it a try? Since we're both out of

practice, we can step on each other's feet and not feel guilty about it." He tried for a lighthearted tone.

After giving the uncrowded dance floor another skim, she caught her lower lip between her teeth. "I suppose one dance would be okay."

He was in too deep to back out now.

Pulse picking up, he stood.

She rose too.

"After you." He motioned toward the dance floor.

He followed her as she wove among the tables, and once on the floor, she turned.

Taking a deep breath, he held out his hand. After a nanosecond hesitation, she took it. Stepped into his arms.

And as he urged her closer with gentle pressure in the small of her back, as they began to move to the music and the scent that was all Kate swirled around him, the world melted away.

It was magic.

And while the dance would last mere minutes, he'd have the memory forever. So on the long, empty nights when he got melancholy, or on those rare occasions he let himself wonder how different his life might have turned out if he'd met someone like Kate a dozen years ago, he could call up the memory of this dance and pretend life had happy endings.

But for right now, he was just going to savor—and enjoy—the moment.

* * *

Being in Eric's arms felt like coming home. There was no other way to describe it.

Which made no sense. She barely knew the man.

Yet there it was.

Not only did they dance in perfect sync, moving effortlessly to the beat of the music, but she felt safe...protected...cherished...as she nestled against his chest, the spicy scent of his cologne hovering in the air as he guided her with a firm but gentle touch through the foxtrot steps.

As far as she was concerned, the dance could go on all night.

But much too soon, the music ended.

Eric didn't release her at once, though—and she made no move to pull back.

However, when the floor began to empty, he at last stepped away. "Thank you for that. I forgot how much I enjoyed dancing." His words came out husky.

"Me too."

"Shall we?" He motioned toward their table.

Left up to her, they'd stay on the dance floor all night.

But Eric had done his duty as a board member and there was no excuse to prolong this up-close-and-personal interlude—or tempt fate.

She nodded and started back toward their seats.

"Eric! I knew you were here somewhere, but it took me awhile to find you in this crowd."

She paused and turned as a mid-fiftyish man in a clerical collar approached.

"Hello, Reverend Jacobs." Eric stopped too. "It's quite a turnout, isn't it?"

"It gets bigger every year, which is gratifying."

"Reverend, meet Sarah's mother, Kate Nolan. Kate, Reverend Carl Jacobs, my minister."

"It's a pleasure, Mrs. Nolan." The man extended his hand, his eyes open and warm and kind. "You have a charming daughter. I was delighted to make her acquaintance when Eric and Anna brought her to services."

"Thank you."

Eric reached inside his jacket and pulled out his phone. Scanned the screen. "Would you two excuse me while I make a quick patient-related call?"

"Of course." Kate moved aside as another couple edged past on their way to the dance floor.

"I'll keep Mrs. Nolan company." The minister turned to her as Eric threaded his way through the crowd and disappeared. "He's a dedicated doctor. His patients are blessed."

"I agree. My daughter is among them."

The band launched into "Unforgettable," and Reverend Jacobs smiled as more people rose and headed toward the dance floor. "Perhaps we should move out of the way before we get trampled. May I walk you back to your table?"

"Yes, thanks."

Once they reached it, the minister spoke again. "Have you and Eric known each other long?"

Since it was obvious her host hadn't shared their history, she motioned for the minister to sit and filled him in. "Without Eric's intervention, my husband would have died that night."

The man's brow crimped. "Eric never mentioned that. But then, he's not the type to blow his own horn. I have to admit I'm a bit confused, though. Eric said you were a widow."

"I am. My husband lived for several months after the accident but never regained consciousness."

Reverend Jacobs's features softened. "I'm so sorry. That had to be a very difficult time for you. Sarah would have been just a baby, I'm sure."

She swallowed past the sudden clog in her throat. "She was

only six weeks old when the accident happened. Somehow I managed to get through the days because I knew she needed me. I didn't think life could get any harder, but when Jack died I felt like part of me died too."

"I know what you mean." A wave of sadness passed through his eyes. "I lost my wife of thirty years to cancer five months ago. The void she left can never be filled."

As his comment hung in the air between them, Kate took a slow breath.

The minister's admission was a reminder that her loss and tragedy weren't unique. That wounded hearts were all around, often hidden behind a bright facade.

"I'm sorry."

"Thank you. It's been a difficult time. But God has sustained me."

She sighed. "I wish I could say the same. I always felt he'd deserted me. I've never understood why he'd take someone like Jack, who was so young and had so much to offer. Or deprive Sarah of a father. It doesn't make sense."

"God's ways can often be difficult to understand. And I certainly don't have all the answers. Nor is this the best place to talk about such issues." He pulled a card from his pocket and held it out. "But I'd be happy to have a conversation about this with you if you'd like to stop by my office. All my contact information is here."

Kate eyed the card.

What could it hurt to tuck it in her purse? Maybe the man could help her make peace with everything that had happened.

It was worth thinking about, anyway.

"Thank you." She took the card.

"You're very welcome. And I see your host is returning." He

motioned toward Eric, who was weaving through the crowd, and stood. "I have several more people to see before I leave tonight. Enjoy the rest of your evening."

She returned the sentiment, and a few moments later Eric rejoined her, brow wrinkled.

"Is there a problem?" She tucked the minister's card in her purse, snapped it closed, and set it back on the table.

"Yes. One of my patients was in an accident, and her parents are on their way to the hospital with her now. I promised to meet them there. In general, I don't intervene in ER situations, but she's got asthma and I thought a familiar face might help calm her down. She's only eight."

"Of course." She picked up her purse again.

"I'm sorry about this. I wanted you to have a pleasant evening."

"And I have. A gourmet dinner, a dessert that exceeded my expectations, even a dance. No complaints on my end."

He exhaled, as if he'd been worried she'd be upset.

A legacy of his relationship with Cindy, no doubt.

"Thanks for understanding." He smiled at her.

"Of course. If I were a parent with an injured child, I'd want *my* doctor there. It's the right thing to do."

"Since the hospital is close to the hotel, would you mind if I call you a cab rather than take you home myself?"

That would be the logical thing to do, but it was barely past eight—and she wasn't ready for this evening to end yet.

"Why don't I go with you?"

He did a double take. "To the hospital?"

Okay. Dumb idea.

She pushed up the corners of her mouth and shrugged. "I was thinking I could extend my evening a bit, but I suppose a hospital isn't the best place to do that."

"Unforgettable" wound down as he scrutinized her. "To tell you the truth, that isn't the way I wanted my evening to end either. If you really don't mind coming with me, I'd appreciate the company. I can always call you a cab from there if this takes longer than I expect."

"That works for me."

His lips bowed. "Thanks for being a good sport. Let's get this done and see if we can still salvage a bit of the evening."

But an hour later, that was looking less and less likely.

Eric had disappeared the minute they arrived, leaving her in the waiting room to play with her phone and page through magazines. She hadn't seen him since.

Just as she gave up hope of any further socializing, the pneumatic door that led to the treatment rooms opened and Eric strode through.

A young couple in one corner rose, and Eric walked toward them. Though they spoke in low tones, their voices carried across the room.

"How is she, Doctor?" Lines of anxiety scored the man's face as he voiced the hoarse question and gripped his wife's hand.

Pressure built behind Kate's eyes.

Waiting for news about someone you loved was wrenching.

"She'll be fine, Mr. Thomas. Let's sit for a minute. Mrs. Thomas?" Eric motioned toward a cluster of chairs and took the mother's arm to guide her there, clearly attuned to the woman's distress.

Astute—and impressive. In a medical world that was often clinical and impersonal, Eric appeared to be an admirable exception.

After they were seated, he spoke again, his tone calm and

reassuring. "Emily has scrapes and bruises, but nothing requiring stitches. Her arm is broken in two places, but they're clean breaks and should heal with no complications. Dr. West is an excellent orthopedic specialist and is with her now. She was having a little trouble breathing when I arrived, but once I got her talking about your vacation to Disney World, she calmed down and her respiration stabilized without the need for medical intervention. We'd like to keep her overnight to make sure she's not in too much pain and monitor her breathing, but I expect she'll be released tomorrow."

The young couple's relief was evident even from across the room.

"I can't thank you enough for coming tonight, Doctor." The mother took his hand, her voice laced with tears. "We told her in the car that you were meeting us, and that helped to keep her calm. We were so afraid she'd have an attack."

"No thanks are necessary, Mrs. Thomas. This is my job."

The girl's father shook his head. "Most doctors don't show up in emergency rooms. This means a lot to us. Especially when it's obvious we interrupted a special event." He waved a hand over Eric's tux.

"I was glad to do it. I'll check on Emily again in the morning, and by lunchtime I expect she'll be discharged. Just tell her not to play soccer quite so aggressively in the future." He flashed them a grin.

"Do you think we should take her off the team?" The man's forehead knotted.

"Not at all. We've got her asthma under control. And kids need to run and play and stretch their wings. Reasonable caution is prudent, but excessive caution is stifling. Sometimes accidents happen, but that's part of living." Eric rose. "They'll be moving her to a room as soon as Dr. West is finished. Let's walk back and get the number so you can be waiting for her when she arrives there."

Eric glanced at her as he ushered the couple toward the treatment area, mouthing, "I'll be right back."

She nodded.

When he reappeared a few minutes later, she rose and met him at the exit, the sliding doors swishing open as they approached.

"Sorry. That took longer than expected. And I didn't contribute much except moral support."

"That counts for a lot in a situation like this."

"I like to think so, anyway." He glanced at his watch as they crossed the dark parking lot, angling it toward an overhead light. Frowned. "It's probably too late to go back to the dinner. Would you like to stop and get a cup of coffee on the way home?"

Yes, she would. But her time in the ER had resurrected too many bad memories, dimming her earlier glow and leaving fatigue in its wake.

"Why don't we call it a night? I had a long week, and I'm sure you did too. There's no reason to keep your mother up any later than necessary."

"Are you certain?" He pressed the autolock for his car.

"Yes. But I had a lovely evening."

He stopped beside the car. Opened her door as he hiked up one side of his mouth. "Well, on the bright side, we may have ended up at a hospital but at least it wasn't because of any broken toes."

She smiled back. "Good point. I think we did quite well for two out-of-practice dancers."

"Just think how much better we'd be if we *did* have a chance to practice."

"True." She slid onto the seat, and a moment later he closed the door behind her.

And closed the door on that discussion.

Yet deep inside, she couldn't help wishing that they *would* have a chance to practice.

But that wasn't going to happen. Tonight had been a one-off.

Amy may have planted a seed during their last conversation about letting go of the past and making a new start, but Eric wasn't the man to make that start with. He'd taken vows, and he'd made no secret of the fact that he was committed to honoring them.

No matter how much she might wish he'd take the advice from his mother and Frank to move on.

6

Kate adjusted the belt on her dress. Ran a brush through her hair. Frowned at herself in the bedroom mirror.

Maybe she should have called and alerted Eric that he and Anna would have two guests for the Sunday service today instead of just one. But he *had* told her she was welcome anytime.

Besides, she hadn't heard from him since the night of the dinner dance a week ago. He'd even sent Anna to the door last Sunday to get Sarah while he returned a patient call—or so Anna had said.

That might be true…but it was also possible he was avoiding her. If he'd felt half the sparks she had during their dance, he could be running scared.

At the ring of the bell, she set her brush down and headed toward the living room, speaking to Sarah as she passed the bathroom. "I'll get that while you finish brushing those teeth."

When she reached the foyer, she took a deep breath, called up a smile, and opened the door. "Good morning, Eric."

"Morning." He gave her a fast sweep. "You're awfully dressed up for grading papers."

"As a matter of fact, if the invitation is still open I thought I'd join you for church today."

His face went blank for a moment, and then a look of—apprehension?—darted through his eyes.

Uh-oh.

She moistened her lips. "I, uh, stopped in to see Reverend Jacobs Friday after school, and we had a long talk. He invited me to attend services, so I decided to come with you today. If that's okay."

"Of course." He gave a slow nod, but the faint creases on his brow sent a different message. "Mom will be delighted."

His mother, not him.

Her stomach bottomed out, and heat flooded her cheeks.

Maybe he felt like she was overstepping after he'd made it clear he had no personal interest in her.

And maybe she was.

Better backtrack.

She swallowed and called up a smile that felt strained around the edges. "You know, this probably isn't the best idea. After all, I have my own car. It isn't as if we have to go together. I don't want to impose and take you out of your way when there's no need. I should have called you earlier and said we'd see you there. I'm sorry to—"

"Whoa." He held up his hand, palm forward. "You just took me by surprise. I'm glad you had a productive chat with Reverend Jacobs."

Whatever reservations she'd spotted in his eyes had vanished—or were now well masked.

"He's an extraordinary listener, with excellent insights. I plan to take Sarah myself to services in the future, but I thought it would be easier to be with people we know on my first visit."

"We can talk about the future later. For today, Mom and I will play host. Hopefully you'll find the service compelling enough to return."

She capitulated—but after today, she and Sarah would go alone. If she decided to return.

Two hours later, however, that was no longer an if. Reverend Jacobs was a captivating preacher, and his warm greeting afterward made her visit feel almost like a homecoming.

"Welcome, Kate." He took her hand in a firm grip, his eyes kind and hospitable. Then he leaned down. "Hello, Sarah. I'm glad you brought your mommy with you today. Did you like the singing?"

"Yes." She gave a shy nod as Kate put an arm around her.

"You know, I bet you'd enjoy our Sunday school." He straightened up to adult height. "The fall session is just getting underway. Sarah would be most welcome."

"Thank you. I saw that on the schedule of youth offerings Anna passed on to me. I'll think about it."

"Give the office a call if you'd like to enroll her."

The four of them moved on so others could greet the minister, and as she reached for Sarah's hand Anna spoke. "You'll join us for breakfast, won't you?"

"Can we, Mommy?" Sarah tipped up her chin, excitement glinting in her eyes.

Kate sent Eric a quick glance, but his face was unreadable. "I, uh, don't want to intrude on your time together."

"Nonsense." Anna waved that aside. "Eric and I would enjoy the company. Right, Eric?" She elbow-nudged him.

"Of course."

"Please, Mommy!" Sarah tugged on her hand. "I could get pancakes."

The temptation to say yes was strong—but if Eric had been less than enthusiastic about her joining them for church, he'd surely prefer they not socialize afterward.

"Not today, honey. I have papers to grade. But thank you for the invitation." She summoned up a smile as she encompassed mother and son in her reply.

95

And the relief in Eric's eyes told her she'd made the wise decision.

Even if it left an empty feeling in the pit of her stomach.

* * *

"Did you and Kate have a misunderstanding?"

At his mother's cut-to-the-chase greeting, Eric adjusted the cell against his ear and angled away from the chart on the laptop in front of him. "Hello to you too, Mom."

"Oh. Sorry. Hello. Well, did you?"

"Did I what?"

"Have a misunderstanding with Kate."

"No."

"Then why won't she go to church with us this Sunday? She stayed for a cup of tea today when she picked up Sarah and told me they'd be going by themselves from now on."

A mixture of relief and regret rippled through him at that news. "There's no reason they shouldn't. We were only taking Sarah as a favor because Kate wasn't attending."

"But it's not that far out of our way to pick them up."

"Mom. Kate is an adult woman fully capable of attending church on her own with Sarah." And sitting beside her in a pew every Sunday was a temptation he didn't need.

"Did you say something that upset her?"

"I haven't even talked to her all week."

"Why not?"

"Why would I?"

A few seconds of silence ticked by. "You know, one of these days someone is going to come along who recognizes and appreciates all of her fine qualities and makes a concerted effort to win her heart."

She was back on the subject of romance.

"I'm not in the market, Mom. And neither is Kate. She's still in love with her husband."

"Of course she is. True love doesn't die." At the catch in his mother's voice, his heart contracted. Yet when she continued, her words were steady. "But that doesn't mean you can't also love someone new."

"I won't argue that point. But it's not an option for me."

A long-suffering sigh came over the line. "Eric, you've been divorced for almost five years. Cindy is remarried. Why spend the rest of your life alone? You should have a wife and family."

"I tried that once. It didn't work."

Another hesitation. "I've never said this before, but I always thought that…well, that maybe you picked the wrong woman the first time around."

He stared at the Lucite Man of the Year award on the credenza across from his desk, bestowed in recognition of his contributions to one of the youth charities he supported.

Outspoken as his mom was, she'd never voiced what he'd always suspected she felt about his marriage—that he and Cindy hadn't been a good match.

And at this stage, there was no sense disputing it.

"Maybe. But it's too late for second-guessing. And I'm not blameless, Mom. I have a demanding career, and it got in the way of our relationship. Marriage and medicine don't seem to mix—at least for me."

"Baloney. Most doctors are happily married. Look at Frank."

The same thing Kate had said.

"He may know some secret I don't."

"There's no secret, Eric. It just takes love and understanding on both sides and a willingness to navigate rocky roads together."

Perhaps.

But all of those had been lacking in his marriage.

He glanced at his watch and stood. "I have to run, Mom, or I'll be behind on my appointments all afternoon."

"This discussion isn't over, you know."

Yeah, he knew.

But as he said goodbye and ended the call, he wasn't going to let his mom make him wish for things he couldn't have.

Even if he was free to marry, saying "I do" again would be a risk even with someone like Kate who seemed sympathetic to the demands of his profession. Midnight calls and interrupted social engagements and missed family events could wear on the most patient person, creating resentment and hurt.

And Sarah's mom had had too much hurt in her life already.

End of discussion.

* * *

Kate read the digital thermometer and caught her lower lip between her teeth.

One hundred and two.

Bad news.

"I don't feel good, Mommy." Sarah shoved off the covers.

Kate smoothed the hair off her daughter's damp forehead, her fingers unsteady. "I know, honey. I'm going to call Dr. Eric. You lie here and rest."

After tucking the covers around her again, Kate strode to the kitchen and placed a call to Eric's exchange. She also phoned Anna to let her know she'd be keeping Sarah home tomorrow.

"I imagine it's a flu bug, Kate." Anna sounded sympathetic but unalarmed after she listened to the symptoms. "Don't worry too much. Children pick up all sorts of viruses, but they bounce back fast. When did she get sick?"

"A couple of hours ago, right before dinner. It came on suddenly. She was fine this morning and had a wonderful time at Sunday school."

"So you *were* there today. I wondered, when I didn't see you at church."

"The later service worked better with the Sunday school schedule." And also allowed her to avoid Eric.

But there was no avoiding him tonight, because after he quizzed her about Sarah's symptoms when he returned her call to the exchange, he insisted on stopping by.

Which meant he was on her doorstep forty-five minutes later, black bag in hand, dressed in worn jeans that hugged his muscular legs and an open-necked blue shirt that matched his eyes, sleeves rolled to the elbows.

She coaxed her lungs to keep inflating and deflating. "Th-thanks for coming by. I didn't think doctors made house calls these days."

"They don't. Nor do I, as a rule. But you sounded really worried."

And he cared enough about her to make the trip.

Warmth filled her.

He may not want to get involved with her personally, but he'd like to.

At least that was the message she took away from his comment.

She backed up and motioned him in. "I appreciate you going above and beyond. Let me take you back to Sarah."

He followed as she led the way down the short hallway and into her daughter's room. "Dr. Eric came to see you, honey."

"Hello, Sarah." He smiled at her as he crossed the room and sat on the edge of the bed. "I heard you were sick."

"Uh-huh. I throwed up."

"The last time was about half an hour ago. After our phone call." Kate moved closer to the bed.

"Well, that doesn't sound like much fun." He opened his bag as he spoke. "Is it okay if I try to figure out what's going on?"

"I guess so. You aren't going to give me a shot, are you?"

His lips quirked. "Not today. I just want to listen to your heart and look in your ears and check out your tonsils."

He chatted with her while he did a quick exam, and when he finished he removed the stethoscope from around his neck and placed it back in his bag.

"Well, little lady, I think you have the flu. But you know what? You should feel much better in a couple of days. In the meantime, I want you to drink a lot of soda and water and juice and take aspirin whenever your mom gives them to you. Will you do that for me?"

"I 'spose." Sarah studied him. "Dr. Eric, do you have a little girl of your own?"

"No." He closed his bag. "But I wish I did."

"Mommy says my daddy watches out for me from heaven now, but I wish I had a daddy who could hold me in his lap and tell me stories. Maybe you—"

"Sarah." Kate's stomach twisted, her voice sharper than she'd intended. Apparently her efforts to be both mother and father to her daughter hadn't been as successful as she'd hoped. "We need to let Dr. Eric go home."

As Sarah gave her a startled look, he picked up his bag and rose. "You rest, young lady. And soon you'll be good as new." He tipped his head toward the door. "Show me out?"

"Yes." She angled toward Sarah. "I'll be back in a minute." She followed him to the foyer, where he turned to her. "One word of advice. Don't ever doubt your parenting skills. Being a one-person show isn't easy, and you're doing a great job." It was almost as if he'd read her mind. And his quiet words went straight to her heart.

She called up a shaky smile. "I think doubts go with the job."

"You can trust the assessment of a neutral third party who's seen a lot of these situations in his practice."

"Thank you for that. Look...could I offer you a cup of tea and a piece of cake? It's the least I can do after you came over here on your day off."

True—but her real motive for extending the invitation was selfish. For somehow, in Eric's calm, in-control presence her doubts and uncertainties evaporated.

But he wouldn't linger. Not after his near panic when she'd told him she was going to church services with—

"If it's not too much trouble, that would be great."

She blinked.

He'd agreed to stay?

Her spirits ticked up.

"Give me a couple of minutes to get Sarah settled, and I'll meet you in the living room."

With a nod, he moved that direction.

Kate returned to her daughter's room, where Sarah gave her an uncertain look.

"Are you mad at me, Mommy?"

"Of course not. Why?"

"You seemed kind of mad when I talked about Daddy."

Kate sat down beside her. Brushed back a damp tendril of hair from her forehead. "I just got sad for a minute because he

101

isn't here with us. He loved you very much, honey. Before you were born we used to plan all the things the three of us would do together. I'm sorry he can't be here to do them with us." Kate picked up the photo of Jack holding Sarah from the bedside table and traced his features. "He's part of you, though. You have his eyes. And you have that little dimple in your cheek, just like he did."

Sarah studied the photo for a moment. "Do you think he misses us up in heaven?"

"I'm sure he does."

"But he can't come back, can he, Mommy?"

"No, honey."

"Do you think he would be mad if I got a new daddy some-time? Just for while I'm down here?"

Kate slowly replaced the photo.

Funny.

She'd always held back from exploring a new relationship because Jack had been her husband.

But he'd also been a father. One who wouldn't want Sarah to grow up without the influence of a kind, caring dad in her life. How many times had they talked about how they wanted her to experience all the joys of a real family—two loving parents and at least a sibling or two? Jack would still want that, even if he couldn't be the one to provide it.

"No, he wouldn't be mad. He'd be happy if you had a father here on earth."

Sarah's brow bunched. "But how would I find one?"

"I'd have to get married again."

"Why don't you do that?"

"Because your daddy was a wonderful man, and it would be hard to find someone like him again."

"Is Dr. Eric like him?"

Kate glanced toward the bedroom door and dropped her voice. "I don't know him well enough to answer that question, Sarah."

Her daughter scooted down in the bed and pulled the covers up to her chin, her eyes drifting closed. "Then I think you should get to know him better."

If only it was that simple.

Kate adjusted the covers. Glanced again at the photo of the man who'd stolen her heart.

It would be unthinkable to do anything that would diminish the beautiful love they'd shared. A love she'd treasure in her heart for always.

But that love was only a memory now...and memories could only sustain a person for so long.

Expelling a breath, Kate turned off the light and stood.

Even if she reached a point where she was ready to move on, however, Eric wasn't available. He'd made that clear. On top of that, after his first disastrous marriage, he truly believed that medicine and marriage didn't mix. So if she decided to consider romance again, she'd have to look elsewhere.

Except that notion held zero appeal.

7

He shouldn't have stayed…but Kate's invitation had been too hard to resist. Especially when she seemed so in need of TLC.

Eric leaned a shoulder against the wall and shoved his hands in his pockets as he listened to the murmur of voices down the hall in Sarah's room.

The words were indistinguishable, other than an occasional higher-pitched reference to "Daddy."

They were talking about Kate's husband.

From all indications, she'd done everything she could to make him as real as possible for Sarah. But that was hard to do when a child had no memory of someone. To her, Jack was only an image, like the characters in her storybooks, with no basis in reality. What she wanted was a real daddy—someone who could hold her hand and share her life.

Bottom line, trying to keep Jack alive for her was a losing battle.

Eric wandered over to the eat-in counter that separated the living room from the kitchen, taking in Sarah's drawings displayed on the refrigerator and a plate of hardly touched dinner beside the sink, along with the items closer at hand—a pile of half-graded school papers, a copy of the church bulletin…and a loan statement reflecting a six-figure balance.

Whoops.

Private material.

He glanced away and took a step back.

But it was hard to unsee that dollar amount.

No doubt it represented Jack's medical bills. Most likely charges from the extended-care facility where he'd spent his last months.

Another case where insurance had only covered certain expenses, leaving the survivors deep in debt.

And based on a reasonable estimate of Kate's salary, it would take her years to repay the loan.

He forked his fingers through his hair. Blew out a breath as his gaze strayed back to the bill.

Sometimes life wasn't fair.

He could write a check for the entire amount and not even miss it. To Kate, the sum would be a fortune.

"She's sleeping now."

He swung toward her as she entered, heat creeping up his neck.

When she glanced at the counter, her own cheeks flushed and she crossed the room, gathered up the papers, and put the statement at the bottom of the stack. "Sorry. The place isn't usually so cluttered."

To pretend he hadn't seen what had been sitting in plain sight would be disingenuous.

"I wasn't looking, Kate. It was just lying there."

Her hands stilled, but she kept her gaze averted. "I know."

"For Jack's care, I assume?"

"Yes." She tapped the papers into a neat stack. "The health insurance covered a significant amount, and the life insurance helped—later. But the expenses piled up fast, and the debt was staggering. It still is." She set the papers on the far side of the counter, shoulders slumping. "Worst of all, there's nothing to show for it. Jack died anyway." Her voice choked.

It took every ounce of his willpower to restrain the urge to pull her into his arms and give her a hug. "I wish the outcome had been different."

"Me too." A few beats passed, and then she straightened and looked at him. "Let me get you the cup of coffee and cake I promised."

"Maybe you could finish your dinner while I indulge in cake." He motioned toward the almost untouched plate in the kitchen.

She shrugged. "I had enough. My appetite's iffy these days."

When she circled the counter and moved into the kitchen, he followed her. "You shouldn't skip meals. I have a feeling your body mass index is in the red zone on the underweight side."

She flashed him a smile as she put a pod in the coffeemaker. "Is that a professional opinion?"

"No. It's twenty-twenty vision and an observant eye."

She pulled two plates from the cabinet and filled a mug with water. "I eat when I'm hungry."

"Do you rest when you're tired?"

She froze for a nanosecond, then slid her mug into the microwave. "I rest when there's time."

"Why do I think that's never?"

Her lips contorted into a wry twist as she cut them each a piece of cake. "You sound like my mother. That's something she would have said."

She was comparing him to her mother?

Hardly.

As his gaze hovered on the ebony hair tumbling around her

face, then moved on to her generous lips and impossibly long lashes, his feelings were *not* motherly.

"You're the only mother in this room, Kate." He cleared the huskiness from his voice. "And father too, for that matter. You're doing an admirable job playing both roles."

"I appreciate the encouragement." Silence fell as she retrieved her mug and his coffee. Set them on the counter, beside the cake. Added a tea bag to her hot water. "But as you picked up from Sarah, I'm not cutting it as a father. And she doesn't feel any link to Jack."

"It's difficult for kids to connect with someone who's not tangible."

"I know. Have a seat." She waved him to a stool and claimed the one beside him. "I've shown her videos and photos and told her stories. I've tried as hard as I can to make Jack real for her. But it's a challenge when someone doesn't have even the glimmer of a memory of a person." She poked at her cake, lips drooping.

There wasn't much he could say to counter that, because it was true.

"He would have been proud of all you're doing to give her a loving home, though."

That also was true.

She flashed him a smile, but the slight sheen in her eyes suggested her emotions were close to the surface. "Thanks for that too." She broke off a bite of her cake with the side of her fork.

As silence fell between them, he picked up his mug. Took a slow sip, buying himself a moment to regroup.

Because *his* emotions were close to the surface too, and his usual rock-solid self-control was wavering as he sat beside this woman who was so in need of a caring touch.

"That's my chore for later." Kate motioned to the stack of school papers. "I try to do grading and lesson plans after Sarah goes to bed so I don't have to give up any time with her."

"Does sleep enter into the equation anywhere? For you, not for Sarah."

"I catch up on my sleep in the summer. But next summer I may see if I can line up a part-time job somewhere. Try to put a bigger dent in the loan balance."

He took a bite of cake. "I get the feeling you're the kind of woman who never gives herself a break."

Her lips curved up as she swirled her tea bag while the water turned amber. "Jack would have agreed with you. He always said I was too intense. That I took everything too seriously. But that's how I'm wired."

"Not a bad thing, as long as you don't overextend."

"Says the man who's on how many boards? Who works how many hours? Who leaves how many black-tie dinners to visit an ER because a patient and her parents need him?" The gentle chiding in her voice was tempered with a touch of humor.

"Now you sound like *my* mother." He took another bite of cake.

"For the record, I'm not being critical. I get that mindset. If I commit to something, I can't do it halfway. Like teaching. Even though I would have preferred to stay home with Sarah, once I accepted that I had to teach again I vowed to give one hundred percent."

"Your students are lucky. So is your daughter."

"Raising her is my number one job. That's why I spend every spare minute with her and do my take-home work at night." She lifted her mug and cocked her head. "But finding balance is hard."

"Tell me about it." He sighed. Set his fork down. Shook his head. "Sometimes I wonder if—"

He snapped his jaws closed.

Kate was much too easy to talk to.

But with all her issues, she didn't need someone dumping their own angst on—

All at once, Kate reached over and touched the back of his hand, sending a high-voltage charge through him. "I have a feeling you're being too hard on yourself about…the past." Her voice was gentle. Filled with compassion.

He focused on her hand. On the warmth of the simple skin-to-skin contact. On the innocent touch that reminded him how lonely and empty his life had become.

Then, calling up every ounce of his self-discipline, he carefully disengaged from her on the pretext of reaching for his fork.

Because a touch like that could make him want things he shouldn't have and tempt him to do things he shouldn't do.

"How did we get into such a heavy discussion?" He speared another bite of cake and slid it into his mouth, lightening his tone.

"I don't know. I think we started off talking about food."

Thank goodness she'd followed his lead.

"Let's get back to that topic. This cake is wonderful. Did you make it?"

"Yes."

"The only time I ever have home baking is at Mom's. I could live on this cake. What is it?" He continued to chow down.

"Sour cream cinnamon streusel coffee cake. It was one of my mom's favorite recipes. Kind of a family standard."

"Well, you can bake this for me anytime. I'd make more house calls if I got treats like this in return."

"So you do make house calls?"

"Once in a great while." He finished off his cake.

"Well, I'm glad you did tonight. I doubt I'd have slept a wink if you hadn't reassured me about Sarah. Although my checkbook might not be too happy when the bill comes." She flashed him a smile.

"There won't be a charge for my visit." No way was he taking money for tonight's call. Not after getting an eyeful of those outstanding medical charges.

Her lips flatlined. "Wait a minute. This was a professional call, Eric. I expect to be billed. You don't owe me any favors. And I always pay my debts."

"I know you do. I saw evidence of that tonight." He'd have to tread carefully. Hurting her pride was the last thing he wanted to do. "I'll tell you what. Bake me one of these cakes sometime and we'll be even."

"That doesn't come close to repaying you for your time."

"Don't undervalue your culinary abilities." He swigged his coffee. "This could be a contest winner."

"As a matter of fact, it was, once upon a time. Mom entered it in some bake-off and won first place."

"There you go."

"Your time tonight is worth more than a cake."

"You can throw in a favor."

"Name it."

"Get more rest. You're doing a great job taking care of Sarah. Now you need to take care of yourself." Maybe then the shadows beneath her lower lashes would fade.

She squinted at him. "How would *you* benefit from that?"

Good question.

And telling her it would give him more peace of mind would be too revealing.

110

He swigged the last of his coffee and propped up the corners of his mouth. "Let's just say I'm trying to save some overworked primary care doctor from having to deal with a patient who succumbed to the flu because fatigue short-circuited her immune system."

It was hard to tell if she bought his explanation, but at least she let it pass.

"All I can promise to do is try."

"That's a start." He rose and picked up his bag. "I should go."

She followed him to the door, leaning past him to open it when they reached the foyer. "Thank you again for coming by."

"Happy to do it. Call me if Sarah gets worse, but I expect the bug will just run its course."

"I hate when she gets sick." Kate drew a shuddering breath. Swallowed. "It always reminds me how fragile life is. How everything can change in the b-blink of an eye."

At the slight stutter in her words and her forlorn expression, his throat thickened.

She looked so alone—and lonely. A kindred soul in many ways. And appealing on more levels than he could count. She was kind, unselfish, caring, dedicated, empathetic, conscientious, loving...not to mention beautiful.

And every instinct in his body was urging him to give her the comfort she seemed to desperately need as she juggled a sick daughter, staggering medical debt, a demanding job, and the myriad responsibilities of single parenthood.

But that would be wrong. And dangerous. Because comfort could be construed as something more...and could also *lead* to something more.

Yet walking away without acknowledging that he understood her fears—and that he cared—also felt all wrong.

So slowly, he reached over. Twined his fingers with hers. Squeezed.

After a moment, she squeezed back.

He didn't say a word.

Neither did she.

But when their gazes met, no words were necessary.

For in her eyes he saw the longing that was in his heart. A longing so intense, so breath-stealing, that for a moment he couldn't move.

Then common sense kicked in.

Starting something he couldn't finish with Kate would do a disservice to them both.

He needed to leave.

Now.

"I'm around if you ever need anything. That's one thing that won't change." The words rasped past his throat.

Her eyes widened a hair, as if she was as surprised by his comment as he was.

But instead of waiting for her to respond, he released her fingers and strode away before he did something really stupid.

Like tug her into his arms, hold her close, and taste her sweet lips.

* * *

That was odd.

As Eric flipped through his mail three days later, he frowned at the return address on the small envelope.

In the years since his divorce had been finalized, his former sister-in-law had never gotten in touch.

Why was Elaine reaching out now?

He closed the mailbox, strode back up the driveway, and unlocked the door that led from his garage to the kitchen. After tossing the rest of the mostly junk mail on the counter, he slit the envelope, withdrew the single sheet of paper, and scanned the note.

Eric:

I know you and Cindy didn't part on the best of terms, but I thought you might want to know that she died a month ago. She was diagnosed with lung cancer last year—so far along that it was hopeless from the start. I guess her chain-smoking finally caught up with her.

Cindy never talked much about the divorce, although she did tell me it was her idea. I loved my sister, but I was well aware of her faults and always thought she made a mistake when she left you. Based on what I know of you from our interactions during your marriage, I can only imagine how devastating that was for you.

I hope life has treated you more kindly since the breakup, and I wish you all the best in the future.

Eric closed his eyes. Took a deep breath as he digested the news.

Cindy was dead.

Even as the words echoed in his mind, they refused to register.

Slowly he lowered himself to a kitchen chair, an image of his wife on their wedding day forming in his memory. She'd

113

looked radiant in all her blond beauty as she'd walked down the aisle to meet him, and his heart had overflowed with love and dreams of a happily-ever-after.

But that happy ending had never come to pass.

Instead, his dreams had disintegrated over the next few years, then imploded the night of the accident that had changed Kate's life forever.

He wiped a hand down his face as the sequence of events he rarely thought about replayed in his mind.

The icy sleet pricking the back of his neck as he'd worked on Kate's critically injured husband.

The icy reception he'd gotten from Cindy after he'd returned to the car—and again later, when he insisted they cut their evening short.

And the icy news she'd delivered on the drive home.

Resting his elbows on the table, Eric propped his head in his hands while the scene in the car replayed in his mind as if it had happened yesterday.

"I can't believe how you hustled me out of there." Cindy *folded her arms and wedged herself into the corner, as far from him as possible. "We didn't even get to eat dinner."*

He started the car. Backed out of the parking spot. "I couldn't handle all the idle chitchat tonight, Cindy. Not after the accident. It seemed so shallow. And the smoke was making me nauseous."

She uttered a cringe-worthy expletive. "Why do you have to take everything so personally? You did your best. More than you needed to. Why can't you just walk away? It's only a job."

An image of the accident materialized in his mind. The woman's devastated face. The man's mangled body. How could

Cindy not understand, after all the years they'd been married, that walking away wasn't in his DNA? "It's more than that to me."

She reached for her purse and extracted a cigarette. Lit it and inhaled deeply. "We need to talk."

Yes, they did. But he was too tired tonight for the kind of discussion she had in mind. "Tomorrow."

"No. Now."

At an odd note in her voice, he looked over at her. When her gaze flickered away, he frowned. Tightened his grip on the wheel.

Whatever Cindy had on her mind was going to change their relationship forever. He could feel it in his gut. And he didn't want to deal with that tonight.

"I'd prefer to table this until tomorrow. I'm not up for a serious discussion."

"This has waited too long already." She took another drag on her cigarette. Exhaled, filling the car with noxious fumes that exacerbated his growing nausea. "Look, I'll cut to the chase. This isn't working anymore, if it ever did. We both know that. Our marriage was a mistake from the beginning. We're not a good match. You can't have enjoyed these past eight years any more than I have."

Eric swallowed. "We took vows before God, Cindy. We can't just toss them aside. Remember 'for better, for worse'?"

She gave a brief, bitter laugh. "I know all about the 'for worse' part. When do we get to the 'for better'?"

That hurt. They'd had interludes of happiness, at least in the beginning. "We had some good times."

"A few. But not enough to justify continuing this relationship. And I want more, Eric. In this marriage I'll always be competing for your attention with a bunch of sick kids. And I'm tired of losing."

"You knew I was a doctor when you married me."

"I thought you were going to be a surgeon, with decent hours most of the time. I didn't know you were going to turn into the pediatric version of Marcus Welby, always on call, always ready to jump every time some kid had a runny nose."

He clenched his teeth. Cindy had always made her opinion clear on his choice of specialty, but never in such hateful language. "Kids matter as much as adults."

"Whatever." She gave a dismissive wave. "The point is, this isn't working. I think we should agree to call it quits and go our separate ways."

"You mean get divorced."

"Yes."

All at once a niggling suspicion coalesced in his mind. "Why wait until now if you've been unhappy for so long?"

A few beats passed as sleet started to ping against the car again in the darkness. "You want the truth?"

No.

But they'd come too far down this road to backtrack.

"Yes."

She leaned over and tapped the ash off her cigarette into the dashboard tray she'd insisted he pay extra for when he'd bought the car. "Okay. I've met someone with potential, and I want to be free to explore that."

His stomach knotted as he posed the question he didn't want to ask. "Are you having an affair?"

"Not yet."

But she'd start one if he didn't agree to a divorce.

How on earth had they reached this dismal stage?

"Look, Eric, it's not that bad." Her tone was less strident now. More placating. "Lots of marriages fail. This way we can

both be free to try to find someone who's more compatible."

"I married for life, Cindy."

"I thought I did too. But it didn't work out."

"Why don't we try counseling?" A suggestion he'd made before, without success.

And she was no more receptive to that idea tonight. "It's too late for that. I'm sorry, Eric."

But she didn't sound sorry. She sounded almost relieved. As if she'd made up her mind about this long ago and had been waiting to spring it on him.

He let out a slow breath. "Going to counseling would be useless if you're not willing to give it a fair shot. To try."

"I did try. We just weren't meant to be together." She leaned back in her seat, the tip of her cigarette glowing in the dark car like a hot poker. "Maybe you'll find someone who'll make you a better wife."

"I already have a wife. Till death do us part."

Till death do us part.

As Eric stared at the letter from Elaine, those last five words echoed in his heart.

Despite the deep-seated loneliness and episodes of dark despair that had plagued him over the years, he'd remained faithful to that vow.

But now he was free.

What that meant in the long term remained to be seen.

Right now, though, he should spend a moment in prayer for the woman he'd once thought he'd loved.

Yet even as he did so, a soft glow of hope filled his heart as thoughts of Kate intruded on his attempt to commune with the Almighty.

Maybe that made him a bad person.

Maybe his spirits shouldn't feel lighter in the face of someone's death.

Maybe a compassionate man would be thinking about Cindy and all she'd gone through in her battle with that terrible disease instead of a woman who could be poised to fill his tomorrows with joy.

But no matter how hard he tried to focus on his troubled past with Cindy, all he could think about was a potentially bright future with Kate.

God forgive him.

* * *

This was it.

Kate verified the address on the mailbox, pulled up to the curb, and surveyed the small bungalow in the quiet, family-oriented neighborhood where children were riding bicycles and playing fetch with their dogs.

A successful doctor like Eric could surely afford to live in more ostentatious surroundings.

It said a lot about him—and his priorities—that he'd chosen to make his home in this modest community.

As she set the brake and reached for the coffee cake on the seat beside her, her pulse picked up.

He probably hadn't expected her to follow through on his payment suggestion for the house call. And in truth, he may have hoped she wouldn't.

But she needed an Eric fix, and this gave her an excuse to see him again.

Yet after their charged parting on Sunday night, it was hard to predict what kind of reception she'd get.

Two minutes later, when he answered the door looking somewhat dazed, her heart skipped a beat.

Since his stunned expression had been in place when he'd pulled the door open, however, something other than her appearance must have produced it. Something unpleasant.

"Um...is this a bad time?"

"No. Sorry." He shook his head, his eyes clearing even as his forehead puckered. "What are you doing here? Is Sarah all right?"

"She's fine. I dropped her off at church for Christmas pageant practice, and I wanted to stop by on my way home and repay you for the house call." She held out the coffee cake. "But I don't want to interrupt if you're in the middle of something."

He took the cake. "I'm not. I just had some unexpected news. Come in." He stepped aside.

"I don't want to intrude."

"You're not. And I'd welcome the company."

Kate hesitated, but only for a moment. He seemed sincere, so why not linger for a few minutes?

"I can't stay long." She moved past him, into the foyer.

"However long you can spare would be appreciated." He closed the door behind her. "I was about to make coffee. Would you like a cup of tea?"

"If it's not too much trouble."

"No trouble at all." He led the way to the kitchen at the back of the house and motioned toward a sturdy antique wooden table and chairs in a large bay off to one side. "Have a seat."

She complied as he set about making her tea, giving the cheerful, bright space a quick survey. Big windows offered views of a large tree-shaded backyard, and while the room was on the

119

sterile side in terms of decorating, it had great potential. "I like your house."

"Thanks. It's the kind of place I always wanted." He crossed to the table and set plates and forks beside the cake. "I'll let you do the honors." He moved back to the counter.

"Jack and I had a house similar to this when we first moved to St. Louis." Sold after his death to pay medical bills, though.

She quashed that depressing thought as he continued working on their drinks.

"I need to warm it up, but I haven't a clue where to begin. Cindy decorated our condo in West County, and our tastes were worlds apart."

Meaning *his* tastes hadn't mattered in decorating decisions back then?

She left that unsaid, though. Clearly his marriage had had issues on multiple levels.

His gaze strayed to a folded sheet of paper and an envelope on the table as he set her tea down and joined her, mug of coffee in hand.

She flicked a glance at the note.

Could that be the reason for his dazed expression when he'd answered the door?

"You seemed to be kind of in shock when I arrived." She nodded toward the letter, choosing her words with care. "I don't want to pry, but I hope that wasn't bad news."

"More for Cindy than for me. The letter is from her sister. Cindy died a couple of weeks ago."

A shock wave rolled through her.

No wonder he'd seemed shaken.

"May I ask what happened?"

"Lung cancer. She was a heavy smoker." He expelled a

breath and stared into the dark depths of his coffee. "I'm sorry for her and for what might have been, and for all the mistakes we both made. But I don't feel a strong sense of grief. By the end of our marriage, Cindy and I were really no more than strangers."

Pressure built in her throat.

How different his marriage had been from hers. While she and Jack had had occasional disagreements, they'd both been committed to sticking with their marriage no matter what obstacles life put in their path.

Just as she had three nights before, she laid her hand over his. "I can't imagine how empty it must have felt living in a relationship like that."

He met her gaze. "Lonely too."

At the intensity in his eyes, her heart stumbled. "I know all about loneliness." The admission came out in a whisper. But it wasn't a new revelation. She'd shared that with him at Frank's barbecue too.

But this time, he responded differently.

Beneath her fingers, he turned his hand. Grasped hers.

As the warmth of his touch seeped into her skin, she suddenly found it hard to breathe.

Was this a play? A message that he was now free to pursue a new relationship—and she was on his radar?

A tingle of sweet anticipation zipped through her, and she took a steadying breath.

While Amy's contention that it was time to take some proactive steps and move on with her life had merit, an unexpected development...or opportunity...like this was also scary.

So until she figured out how, or if, she wanted to proceed, she needed to play it safe and cautious.

Forcing up the corners of her mouth, she lightened her tone.

"Well, we're not lonely tonight. Let's enjoy the moment and have a piece of cake." She eased her hand free.

He let it go…and he also let her dodge any further personal discussion as they ate their cake and she made a fast exit.

But a day of reckoning was coming. Because Eric seemed like the kind of man who'd go after what he wanted with single-minded determination and diligence.

Meaning that until she decided what *she* wanted, she needed to walk a wide circle around the man who was making her rethink the isolated life she'd been leading for almost six years—and wanting more than she'd allowed herself to believe would ever again be possible.

8

"I hear I have competition in the baking department."
Kate took a sip of her tea and smiled at Anna across the woman's kitchen table. "Hardly."

"I don't know." There was a twinkle in her eye. "Eric raved about your coffee cake. It was nice of you to make one for him, by the way."

"It was the least I could do after he stopped by to see Sarah—and on a Sunday night." Kate leaned back. Exhaled. "This is the perfect antidote to a long, drawn-out teachers meeting. Thanks for watching Sarah later than usual."

"My pleasure. She's a delightful little girl and no trouble at all." Anna glanced out the window toward the patio, where Sarah was engrossed in a make-believe game, taking full advantage of the unseasonably warm weather in the diminishing daylight. "She's so excited about the Christmas pageant at church. It's all she's talked about for the past two days. If you need any help with the angel costume, I'm more than happy to lend a hand."

Kate shook her head. "Speaking of angels—how did I get lucky enough to find you?"

"I'm no angel." She waved that aside, though a faint flush rose on her cheeks. "And it wasn't luck that brought you to me—and vice versa. It was Eric." The doorbell chimed, and Anna rose. "Will you excuse me for a moment, my dear?"

"Of course. We should be leaving anyway." Kate started to get up, but Anna put a hand on her shoulder. "Don't rush off yet. Let Sarah soak up the last of the sunlight." She hurried off without waiting for a response.

Nevertheless, Kate stood and carried her mug to the sink. They needed to leave. Dinner was already going to be far later than usual.

As she rinsed out the mug, Anna reentered the kitchen, Eric on her heels. And he was toting two large white sacks.

"Well, look who stopped by." Anna's feigned surprise was almost comical.

It appeared she'd dusted off her matchmaking hat now that Eric was no longer bound by his marriage vows.

Oh, brother.

This was going to be beyond awkward.

But apparently not for Eric, who sent her a warm smile that zipped straight to her core. "I heard you had to work late tonight. I did too. I thought we could all forego kitchen duties and share Chinese. I brought chicken fingers and fries for Sarah." He lifted one of the white bags.

So he'd been in on his mother's plan.

Yet how could she say no after he'd gone to all that trouble?

Besides, it would be safe as long as Anna was here to deflect any electricity the two of them might generate.

She rubbed her palms down her slacks. "Sarah will love that. It's not a treat she often gets."

"Is Chinese okay for you?" He hefted the other bag.

"Perfect. A treat for me too."

"I'll go get Sarah and collect any toys that are out there." Anna crossed to the back door and let herself out.

Kate gathered up plates and eating utensils while Eric

unpacked the bags. "You're going to spoil us, you know." She tossed the comment over her shoulder.

"You could use some spoiling."

At his husky reply, she almost dropped the glass she'd just pulled from the cabinet.

O-kay.

Unless she was misreading his tone, he was venturing into personal territory. His presence here tonight suggested the same thing. He was making it clear he wanted to spend time with her. Letting her know he was interested in moving their relationship to a different level. One much deeper than friendship.

But was she brave enough to take the leap with him?

"Kate."

At his soft summons, she peeked over at him.

"You're not annoyed at me for showing up tonight, are you?"

Annoyed?

How could she be annoyed when he looked at her with those deep blue eyes and that tender expression?

"No. Just surprised." She managed a strained smile. "Besides, I'm not one to turn down free food."

His gaze never wavered. "My coming tonight is about more than food."

Pretending not to know what he meant would be disingenuous.

She filled her lungs. Tightened her grip on the knives and forks in her hand. "I know."

"The news I got last week changed a lot of things. I'm still struggling with how to juggle a relationship and the demands of my practice, but I'm willing to work on that for the right woman."

Oh, man.

He was laying all his cards on the table.

So in fairness, she needed to do the same.

She glanced out the kitchen window. Anna and Sarah were engaged in an animated conversation that showed no signs of winding down.

Taking a steadying breath, she loosened her grip on the cutlery to restore circulation to her fingers. "I appreciate your honesty. And I'm flattered by your interest. But nothing has changed in *my* world. I'm still struggling with fear and guilt and uncertainties and conflicting loyalties. I'm working on all of those, but it will take time."

"I'm a patient man as long as there's even a sliver of hope for a positive outcome."

She moistened her lips and summoned up her courage. "I think there could be."

A slow smile teased the corners of his mouth. "That's enough for me. May I make a suggestion? Why don't we see each other, but keep it casual? That will give us both a chance to dip our toes into a different kind of relationship, test the waters as we get to know each other, and see where that leads. Does that sound reasonable?"

More than.

She nodded.

The back door opened and Sarah entered, followed by Anna, who gave them a once-over—and a satisfied nod. As if she knew her matchmaking plans were falling into place.

But that was impossible. The woman wasn't a mind reader. She couldn't have—

"How come your face is pink, Mommy?"

At Sarah's question, she flicked a glance at Eric. Lips twitching, he went back to opening cartons of food as more heat flooded her cheeks.

Apparently mind reading wasn't required to discern her emotional state. The physical evidence was sufficient.

"Um…it's kind of warm in the kitchen. You ready for chicken nuggets and fries?" If anything would distract her daughter, that should be it.

"Yes!" She scurried over to the table, climbed on a chair, and struck up a conversation with Eric.

Fortunately, Anna confined her commentary to a few smug looks. And at least she kept the conversation flowing during dinner.

Only after they finished and Kate gathered up her purse and Sarah's accoutrements did Eric speak to her one-on-one again for a brief moment.

"I'll call you. That still okay?"

Even though she was still battling uncertainty, she nodded.

And sent a silent prayer heavenward for guidance—and courage.

* * *

"Okay, partner, we need to have a talk."

Eric swiveled away from his laptop as Frank strode into his office and dropped into the chair across the desk.

"What's up?"

"It's time to add a third physician to this practice."

At least Frank wasn't pestering him with questions about Kate again. Nor had he for a while.

"We've talked about this before."

"I know. And you've always dragged your feet. But we don't have to work twelve-hour days anymore like we did early on to keep the wolf from the door. We have a thriving practice. There's plenty of work for a third doctor. Plus, we'd only have to cover calls every third week instead of every two. With the baby coming, Mary thinks I need to lighten up my work schedule so I have more time to spend with the family. I agree."

Eric leaned back in his chair. "So do I."

"I know you'd prefer to—" Frank closed his mouth. Stared at him. "Wait a minute. What did you say?"

"I said I agree."

"Just like that? No protest? No litany of reasons why this isn't a good time?"

"Nope."

Frank's expression slowly morphed from incredulous to calculating. "I bet I can guess the reason for your change of heart in one word. Kate. Things are heating up, aren't they?"

"I wouldn't say that exactly." Even if Friday-night take-out dinners at his mom's had become a regular event, along with Sunday church, followed by breakfast. Supplemented with regular phone calls and an occasional coffee date with Sarah in tow, much to the youngster's delight.

"I knew something was in the wind the day of the barbecue. And it's about time you had more in your life than a job and charity work. I'm happy for you, pal. This third partner will help us *both* out. I bet Kate will be glad if you have fewer interruptions during off hours too."

No doubt that was true, although she'd never complained when duty pulled him away.

Unlike Cindy.

He linked his fingers together. "Do you have someone in mind?"

"Yes. Carolyn Clark."

Ah. The hard-working pediatric resident with excellent educational credentials who'd impressed him during her brief stint at their practice.

"She'd be a good fit, from what I've seen. Do you think she'd be interested in joining us?"

"Yep. I already made a few discreet inquiries."

"Let's talk to her, then."

Frank scratched his head. "I thought I was going to have to do a hard sell with you about this. I owe Kate big time." He leaned back and crossed an ankle over a knee. "So how goes it with her? I want details."

Eric tapped a finger on the arm of his chair as something his mother had said to him weeks ago about his partner's ability to balance marriage and medicine replayed through his mind.

Why not pick Frank's brain and try to tap into his recipe for success?

"Can I ask you something?"

"Sure. Shoot."

"It's no secret that Cindy and I made a mess of our marriage. And one of the biggest problems was my career. She hated how it intruded on our personal life. I was never able to figure out how to balance the two. But you seem to manage fine."

Frank's eyes narrowed. "Can I be honest?"

"When have you ever not been?"

"Ha ha. But I've tried to be discreet in terms of your marriage because you were always so closemouthed about it. However…the problems Cindy had with your career weren't a hundred percent your fault. I'll concede you can be driven at times. But doctors who are serious about the Hippocratic oath always serve two masters. Yes, we love our families, but we also have an obligation to our patients, whose lives are literally in our hands. You don't have to marry a doctor to realize that. Cindy knew what she was getting into. Don't beat yourself up about that. She just wasn't willing to play second fiddle—ever. I think that reflects more on her than on you."

Much as he wanted to take Frank's opinion at face value, his doubts went too deep and were of too long a duration to be dispelled so quickly.

"But wouldn't most spouses be upset when their partner's professional obligations interfere with their plans as a couple? Doesn't Mary ever resent the disruptions caused by your job?"

"No. Which doesn't mean she isn't disappointed now and then when my job interferes with our life. But she knows I do everything I can to make time for us as a couple—like pushing for a third partner." He flashed him a grin. "So we've never had any problems."

Eric turned his pen end to end on the desk. "I wish I could be certain it would work like that for me."

Frank stood, his demeanor serious. "It can. I don't know Kate very well, but I liked what I saw. Cindy's gone now. There's nothing except fear to keep you from moving forward. Not to get sloppy or anything, but I know how conscientious you are. And caring. If you couldn't make your marriage work, nobody could. My advice? Don't let one bad experience hold you back if you've met someone who's a better fit."

As his partner exited, Eric leaned back in his chair.

He couldn't fault anything Frank had said.

And Kate was definitely a better fit than Cindy, from all indications.

But she was as gun-shy as he was.

So unless they could both find a way to overcome their doubts and fears, the tentative groundwork they'd been laying for a deeper relationship could deteriorate as fast as a patient in desperate need of life-giving oxygen.

* * *

Anna handed over another straight pin, then backed up and surveyed the hem of Sarah's angel costume. "I think that will do it. I'll run it up for you on the machine tomorrow, Kate."

Kate rose from her kneeling position and lifted Sarah down from the sturdy chair in Anna's kitchen, giving her a hug as she lowered her to the floor. "You're a beautiful angel, honey."

"Are we going to make the wings next week?"

"Yes. Dr. Eric said he'd stop at the hardware store for the wire we need for the frame."

"Mommy's been working on the wreath for my hair at night after I go to bed." Sarah angled toward Anna. "It's really pretty."

"I think you'll be the loveliest angel ever." Anna patted her head. "Now let's get that robe off so it stays clean. Angels always look neat and tidy."

Once Kate lifted the garment over Sarah's head and her daughter scampered off to play, she sent Anna a grateful smile. "I can't thank you enough for all your help. I feel like Sarah has a new grandmother."

Anna took the robe and draped it over the back of a chair. "That's a role I've always wanted to play. And I love taking care of her. It's given me a new sense of purpose. I still miss Walter every day, of course, but the loss is easier to bear, knowing you and Sarah are counting on me."

"This arrangement has truly been a blessing all around."

"Indeed it has." Anna closed the pin box and turned, faint furrows etching her brow. "I may have a small glitch in our scheduling, though."

"I'm sure we can work around it. What's up?"

"I know this is short notice, but my cousin called last night.

She and a friend were planning to go on a cruise the week of Thanksgiving, but her friend had to back out. She asked me to go instead. I've always wanted to take a cruise, and this seemed like a providential opportunity. But if I say yes, I wouldn't be able to watch Sarah on Monday and Tuesday of Thanksgiving week. And I hate to disrupt her routine after all the upheaval she's had in her life."

Anna was hesitating about the cruise because she was worried about Sarah?

Caring and thoughtful didn't begin to describe Eric's mother.

"Of course you have to say yes." Kate faced her. "You can't pass up such a wonderful opportunity. And Thanksgiving is still two weeks away. I have plenty of time to make other arrangements. Sarah will be fine for two days with someone else."

"I had a feeling you'd say that. So I spoke with my neighbor earlier today. She's a lovely young woman, very responsible, with two small children of her own. Sarah's played with them on occasion. She said she'd be happy to fill in for me. I know you're leaving for your sister's on Wednesday, and I'll be back Sunday night. So I'll only miss two days."

"Don't give it another thought. Just have a wonderful time."

"I plan to. Although I do hate leaving Eric alone for the holiday. He and Walter and I always spent Thanksgiving together. But he assured me he'd be fine by himself, so I suppose I shouldn't fret. Besides, he'll probably go to Frank's."

Kate frowned.

No, he wouldn't. Eric had told her last night that his partner was having Thanksgiving dinner at his in-law's house in Illinois.

So where would Eric eat *his* turkey?

"Is something wrong, dear?" Anna touched her arm.

Kate called up a smile. "No. I was just thinking how Thanksgiving will be here before we know it."

No need to mention the idea that had just popped into her head.

Especially since she wasn't sure she'd pursue it, anyway.

But later that night, as she lay in bed, she reached a decision.

And unless something changed her mind in the next twenty-four hours, she was going to follow her heart and take a chance.

* * *

"Hi, Amy." Kate pressed the cell to her ear and sank onto the couch. With Sarah coloring in her bedroom, the coast should be clear for the conversation she wanted to have with her sister.

"Kate? Isn't it my turn to call for our Sunday afternoon chat?"

"Yes, but Eric is stopping by in a little while and I didn't want to have to cut our session short. Are you in the middle of something?"

Amy snorted. "Just the usual mayhem."

"What's going on now?"

"A friend of Cal's went overseas for a couple of weeks and somehow conned my good-natured husband into babysitting his iguana. The twins are fascinated. Personally, when it comes to pets I prefer the warm, cuddly variety. However, as long as I don't have to touch it, I suppose I can put up with a reptile in my house for a limited time. Sorry you and Sarah will have to endure our scaly friend while you're here for Thanksgiving."

Their visit was the very subject she wanted to talk about.

Kate took a deep breath. "Speaking of that…Anna told me on Friday that she's going on a cruise over Thanksgiving. So Eric will be alone for the holiday. I don't want to impose, and I know he's a stranger to you, but—"

"Invite him to join us."

Kate smiled.

Her sister had responded exactly as she'd expected.

"Are you certain?"

"Of course. One more mouth to feed in this household won't even be noticed. And there's plenty of room. We'll kick out the iguana if we have to. Plus, I already have a ginormous turkey in the freezer. If Eric likes dark meat, he may have to fight the twins for the legs, but he sounds like an amenable guy."

Kate tucked her feet under her, mouth curving up. "He is."

"Also very special if you're inviting him to spend Thanksgiving with the family."

She plucked at a loose thread on the couch. "I'd feel bad about *anyone* spending Thanksgiving alone. Inviting him is the charitable thing to do."

A beat ticked by. "So he's a charity case. Right." Of course her sister saw through her lame rationale.

"He's also special." May as well admit the truth. "But at the moment, we're in the friendship stage. I told him I need time and space, and he's on board with that."

"Kudos to him. And for the record, you're worth waiting for. I'm glad he recognizes that. I can't wait to meet this guy."

"He might not come."

"He'll come."

"How do you know?"

"Instinct."

"I have to work up the courage to ask him first."

"You will. And if you don't, *I'll* ask him."

Kate gave a soft laugh. "What would I do if I didn't have you to talk to?"

"I feel the same. You were an excellent sounding board when

I needed guidance a few years back. If it wasn't for you, I might never have married Cal and left my glamorous life in Atlanta behind to live in the Smokies and make quilts." She paused. "Wait a minute. Come to think of it…"

As her sister's voice trailed off in mock horror, Kate gave a soft laugh. "You wouldn't trade your life for anything and you know it."

"You're right about that. Listen, you bring that overworked doctor down here and we'll show him a Thanksgiving he won't forget. Just do me one favor. Warn him about the iguana."

* * *

Kate was nervous.

In fact, she'd seemed a bit on edge every time he'd seen her since he'd stopped by a week ago to finish off his weekend with cake and coffee and conversation.

He needed to get to the bottom of this.

As he walked her to the door of her apartment building Sunday morning while Sarah skipped ahead through the chilly November air, he tried to think of a diplomatic way to broach the subject—and prayed she wasn't getting cold feet about the two of them.

"Thanks again for picking us up, Eric. And for breakfast." She sounded a bit breathless as she dug through her purse for her keys.

"It was my pleasure." He hesitated for a moment—but if she had bad news to share, there was no sense putting it off. "Look, is there something wrong? You've seemed kind of tense all week."

She cleared her throat. Glanced at Sarah, who'd been sidetracked by a chipmunk on a tree stump off to the side. "I've, uh, been trying to work up the courage to talk to you about something."

Stomach clenching, he braced. "Okay."

She tucked her hair behind her ear. Moistened her lips. "Since your mom will be on a cruise over Thanksgiving, I wondered if you might like to come with me and Sarah to my sister's for the holiday. I remember you saying once that Thanksgiving in the Smokies sounded appealing. Amy says there's plenty of room, although she did tell me to warn you they're iguana sitting for a friend of her husband's." She finished her rapid-fire recitation in a rush of breath.

The knot in his stomach loosened as his spirits ticked up. "You're asking me to spend Thanksgiving with you and your family?"

"Yes. But I know it's a long trip and they're all strangers to you, so it's okay if—"

"I accept."

Her eyes widened. "Really?"

"Really. I can't think of anywhere I'd rather be on the holiday than with you and Sarah and Amy and her family…and the iguana." He hitched up one side of his mouth.

Her features softened, and at the sudden warmth and longing in her eyes his mouth went dry.

Did she realize the subliminal invitation she was sending?

Likely not.

And much as he wanted to respond—to tug her close, run his fingers through her hair, and taste her lips—this wasn't the time or place. Only when she gave a clear, deliberate green light would that be appropriate.

He cleared his throat. "I'll touch base with you in a day or two to finalize the travel arrangements."

She gave a jerky nod. "That'll work."

After calling goodbye to Sarah, he pivoted and strode away. Fast. Before his self-discipline failed.

Because there were still hurdles to conquer on both sides before they got too involved.

Despite Frank's encouragement, he wasn't yet convinced he could successfully juggle marriage and medicine—although his confidence was growing.

As for Kate...it was clear she was trying to move on. But would she ever be able to really let Jack go and give her heart to someone else?

Unknown.

The invitation to share Thanksgiving with her family was a positive sign, though.

And perhaps during their time together in the Smokies, both of them could find a way to make peace with their pasts and take an exploratory step into the future.

9

From the passenger seat beside him, Kate glanced over her shoulder at Sarah, whose excited, nonstop chatter had at last been silenced by sleep.

Eric smiled. "The sandman finally won."

She shifted her attention to him. "Thanks for being so patient with her. I'm sure you would have preferred a quieter drive."

"To tell you the truth, most of my drives are *too* quiet."

"Well, this one wasn't. Sarah doesn't usually get so wound up. But she was awake at dawn, ready and waiting to leave."

"Which means her mother was awake at dawn too." No wonder Kate had faint shadows under her eyes.

She shrugged. "I had things to do anyway."

"You must be tired. Why don't you grab a few z's? According to my phone, we're still an hour out."

"I don't know if I could drift off like Sarah did. I'm as excited about this visit as she is. I can't wait to have an in-person conversation with Amy." She angled toward him. "I hope you two hit it off."

"Goes without saying if she's anything like you."

"She's not. Amy's always been more outgoing and self-confident. A take-charge kind of person in the best sense of the term. She's a doer and an organizer, and she always has things under control. Unlike me."

Eric shook his head. "Don't sell yourself short."

Kate sighed and gazed out the window, into the darkness. "'In control' isn't a term I'd apply to my life in recent years."

"I disagree. The things that happened to you were *beyond* your control, but you coped well under difficult circumstances. And through it all you've been an exceptional mother. You deserve a huge amount of credit for that."

"Thanks for the kind words." She clapped a hand over her mouth as a yawn snuck up on her. "Sorry."

"You won't insult me if you take a catnap."

"I suppose I could close my eyes for a few minutes if you don't mind."

"Not at all."

She settled back into the corner of his car, and within five minutes her even breathing indicated she'd succumbed to sleep.

An hour later, when he turned onto the drive that led to her sister's cabin, she was still out cold.

The crunch of tires on the gravel, however, not only awakened her, it announced their arrival. As he pulled up in front of the cabin and set the brake, the front door was flung open, revealing a silhouetted, jeans-clad woman.

Kate straightened up. "Sorry. I didn't mean to conk out."

"No worries. The welcoming committee is out." He motioned toward the cabin.

Her mouth bowed. "Amy's been watching for us."

Before Eric could respond, the woman called over her shoulder, then raced down the steps, bypassing the last one with a leap. Kate pushed open her door, and the sisters met in front of the car, clinging to each other in a tight hug.

"It's so good to see you." Amy's voice was muffled as he slid from behind the wheel.

"Same here. I've missed you so much."

Eric remained beside the car as he watched the reunion. Though it was difficult to see much in the dim light from the porch, there were some obvious physical differences between the sisters. Amy was taller than Kate, and her hair wasn't as dark. While Kate was softly rounded in all the right places, Amy's build was more angular and athletic. And her outgoing, no-holds-barred greeting suggested a more boisterous, impulsive nature than Kate's.

But whatever their physical or personality differences, it was clear the sisters shared a strong emotional bond.

When the hug ended, Amy crossed to him and extended her hand. "Eric, I presume. Welcome."

He returned her firm grip. "Thank you for inviting me. I'm looking forward to being part of your holiday."

Amy planted her hands on her hips. "I hope you still feel that way when you leave on Sunday. Kate did tell you about the iguana, right?"

"Yes. I've been duly warned about your temporary guest."

"*Very* temporary. We're eccentric enough without having strangers think we gravitate toward unusual pets. I'm sure you'll be happy to know that Wally isn't sleeping in your room." She rolled her eyes. "The next time Cal agrees to—"

"Did I hear my name mentioned?" A tall, dark-haired man came out the front door and joined them.

"You did. We were discussing Wally."

Cal slipped his arm around Amy's shoulders and grimaced. "Why do I think I'll never hear the end of this?"

"Because you won't." She grinned and gave him a hip bump. After taking care of the introductions, she peeked inside the car. "Looks like someone nodded off."

"About sixty miles ago." Kate spoke from across the car roof as she circled around to the rear door beside the booster seat.

"I'm sure you're *all* exhausted after that long drive. Are you hungry?" Amy encompassed both of them in her question.

"We stopped for dinner along the way." Kate leaned down, nudged Sarah awake, then unbuckled her.

"In that case, let's get you all settled. We can visit tomorrow."

By the time the luggage had been brought in, towels distributed, and Sarah and the twins were rolled into sleeping bags in the great room, it was after nine.

"You should be fine in the twins' room, Kate. And I hope the sleeper sofa in the den is okay for you, Eric." Amy gave him a rueful look. "I know it's not the Ritz."

"Trust me, the sofa will be far more comfortable than some of the places I racked out during my residency." Cal grinned.

"Thanks for being a good sport. Is there anything else either of you need tonight?"

"No. You go get some rest yourself." Kate shooed her off.

Amy wrinkled her nose. "Like that will happen. Believe it or not, Caitlin still likes a midnight bottle." She angled toward him. "My six-month-old."

"A healthy appetite is a good sign."

"I'll remind myself of that while I'm feeding her in the wee hours. Good night, you two." She disappeared up the rough-hewn split-log stairway, leaving him alone with Kate in the dim, quiet house.

"Sleep well." He spoke softly to keep from disturbing the three kids who were slumbering in front of the fireplace on the other side of the room.

"I usually do when I'm here. I like being in the country."

141

"Me too. And this is a perfect spot to celebrate the holiday. Thanks again for inviting me."

She gave a soft laugh. "Save your thanks until we leave. It can get pretty crazy around here with all the kids."

"It's a good kind of crazy, though." He shoved his hands into the pockets of his jeans. "And it's nice to be in a home so filled with love. It's also heartwarming to see such a happy family— and such a successful marriage."

"They do happen. I speak from experience."

"I know." He let out a slow breath. "The question is whether you—"

He clamped his lips shut.

This wasn't the place to voice the concern that had been plaguing him for weeks. Only time would tell whether she was willing to give love a second try. And pushing her to make the decision before she was—

"Whether I what?" Her voice was soft, her expression difficult to read in the dim light. But an almost palpable yearning emanated from her.

Too potent to ignore.

Instead of answering her question, he withdrew one of his hands from his pocket. Lifted it. Traced the curve of her cheek, his touch whisper-soft against her satiny skin.

Her sharp intake of breath spoke volumes. But rather than step back, she swayed toward him.

Locking gazes with her, he gave up the fight and slowly leaned down. One taste of her lips, that was all he wanted tonight. One quick, sweet taste to—

"Oh, I'm glad you're both still up. I forgot—"

He jerked back as Amy paused halfway down the steps.

Kate's sister cleared her throat. "I, uh, just wanted to let you

142

know we plan to go to services tomorrow morning at ten if that's okay with you two."

"Th-that's fine. Thanks." Kate edged back from him.

"Great. Good night again. This time for good." Amy disappeared back up the stairs. A few seconds later a door clicked shut.

Silence descended.

But the moment was lost, the mood broken.

And maybe that was for the best.

They were both tired after the long drive, and fatigue-fueled late-night kisses stolen in the dark might be regretted in the light of day.

"I guess we should call it a night." He once more shoved his hands deeper into his pockets in case they were tempted to misbehave again.

"Right." She backed away. "I'll see you in the morning. I hope you have a restful sleep." And then she fled up the stairs.

Restful sleep?

Fat chance after that almost-kiss.

But as he turned and wandered down the hall toward the study, one thought consoled him.

If Kate had been receptive to a kiss tonight, maybe her resistance would crumble again in the not-too-distant future.

Assuming *he* didn't end up getting cold feet.

* * *

Their Thanksgiving visit to the Smokies was everything Kate had hoped it would be—except for one thing.

She and Eric had zero privacy.

They'd come for family time, and Amy and Cal had given them that in spades.

143

Thanksgiving started with a boisterous pancake breakfast, continued with the church service, then segued into dinner preparations—a whole-family effort. Amy even recruited Eric to peel potatoes, claiming that if he could handle a scalpel, he could manage a paring knife. After cleanup, they paid their respects to Wally, admired the gazebo Cal was building among the rhododendrons at the back of the property, and stayed up late playing board games.

Friday was equally packed with activities, and Amy was up till all hours with a fussy Caitlin, which wasn't conducive to privacy.

On Saturday Cal took them into Great Smoky Mountains National Park for a tour.

As they wandered down a path by a crystal-clear stream, the children up ahead while Cal and Amy strolled arm in arm and Caitlin slept in a carrier on Cal's back, Eric slowed his pace and sent her a wry grin. "Alone at last."

She shook her head. "Hardly."

"Why do I think this is as good as it's going to get while we're here?"

Well, shoot.

Was he regretting his decision to join her for the holiday?

"I'm sorry, Eric. It's been a bit of a whirlwind, hasn't it?"

"Don't apologize. I've enjoyed being part of your family's celebration." He nodded toward Amy and Cal. "I don't want to put you in an awkward position if you're trying to play our relationship low-key, but would they be surprised if they turned around and saw us holding hands?"

Her heart picked up speed. "After what Amy interrupted Wednesday night?" She wasn't going to play games and pretend they hadn't almost kissed, even if they'd had no chance to talk about it.

"Her timing wasn't the best. Or maybe it was, depending on your perspective."

In the past three days, she'd debated that very thing—and come to a conclusion that was only fair to share with Eric. "From my perspective, it stunk."

At her frank reply, he barked out a laugh that drew an over-the-shoulder glance from her sister. Then he reached over, took her hand, and laced his fingers with hers. "May I say that's music to my ears?"

A tingle ran down her spine as the warmth of his fingers chased away the chill in the mountain air. "You may."

"Does that mean you're willing to pick up where we left off on Wednesday night once we have a little privacy?"

"Don't count on that down here."

"I won't. But we'll be back in St. Louis tomorrow, and—"

"Mommy! Come see the fish!" As Sarah raced toward her, grabbed her free hand, and towed her toward a pool in the stream up ahead, she sent Eric a contrite glance.

He grinned, shrugged, and fell in behind them.

The man had the patience of Job. It had been one interruption after another since they'd arrived.

But in truth, *this* interruption wasn't unwelcome.

Because while the notion of picking up where they'd left off on Wednesday was exhilarating, it was also scary.

And now that she'd more or less given him the green light, she needed a little space to think about all that would mean—and make certain she was ready to take such a big step.

* * *

"Knock, knock. You still up?"

As Amy's voice pulled her back from the edge of sleep in the twins' room, Kate flipped on the light, threw back the covers, and padded over to the door.

Amy stood on the other side holding two mugs of hot chocolate.

"I gave up on you." Kate yawned and squinted at her watch. "When you said you were going to stop by after everyone was settled for the night, I didn't think you meant ten-thirty."

"Sorry." She entered the room. "Caitlin was fussy. Again." She handed over a mug and continued across the room, sipping her drink as she sat on the edge of the twin bed that wasn't being used.

Kate returned to her bed, pausing to swipe off a few flecks of whipped cream from beside her sister's mouth. "It's nice to see that some things never change." She held up her cream-bedecked finger.

"Ha ha." Then Amy's expression grew melancholy. "Too bad other things do, though."

Kate sobered too. "You're thinking about Mom, aren't you?"

"I have been all weekend. It was strange not to have her here for Thanksgiving. It's like a puzzle with a missing piece."

"I hear you. She was always such a rock."

"I know. I feel kind of like a ship adrift without an anchor now that she's gone. On top of everything else, I missed her gravy at dinner. No one made it like Mom."

"That's true." Kate took a sip of her cocoa. "You'll think I'm crazy when I tell you this, but sometimes I talk out loud to her. Like she's still there."

"If you're crazy, I am too because I do the same thing. I miss her every day. But it has to be doubly hard for you, since she was part of your daily life."

"I won't pretend it hasn't been tough. But meeting Anna

helped. It's not the same as having Mom, of course, but in many ways she reminds me of her. And she's taken Sarah and me under her wing. It was a godsend that she came into our lives when she did. Thanks to Eric."

Amy watched her over the rim of her mug as she took another sip. "Speaking of Eric…I know you said you were just friends, but I have to say things didn't look too platonic the other night when I interrupted you two. And did I spot a bit of hand-holding in the park today?"

"It's been platonic until this weekend." She wrapped her fingers around the toasty mug. "But I think that may be about to change."

"Good. I like what I've seen of him these past few days. And he and Sarah seem to have hit it off."

"They have. The trouble is, I still love Jack."

"We already had this discussion."

"I know, but I'm still struggling to reconcile how I can love two different men."

"How does a mother love more than one child? The heart has an infinite capacity for love, Kate. We all love many people in our lives, in different ways. The love you have for Jack will always be there, and part of your heart will always belong to him. But that doesn't mean there isn't room for someone else. Love Eric for himself—for all the special qualities that are unique to him. That won't diminish in any way the love you have for Jack. It's just different. A new dimension of love, if you will."

Kate let out a slow breath. "You always know what to say."

"No, I don't. But I know you. And I know you deserve to be happy again. I also know that's what Jack would want. You just have to let go and take a leap of faith."

"What if I fall flat on my face?"

"Not gonna happen."

"How do you know?"

"Because Eric will be there to catch you."

Kate tucked that notion into her heart. "I like your take."

"Then let's toast to that, drink up, and go to bed or we'll both be zombies tomorrow."

They clicked mugs, and less than five minutes later her sister slipped through the door, leaving her alone.

But if Amy was right, and if she summoned up the courage to follow her heart, she might not be alone for long.

* * *

What was that annoying noise?

As the odd sound intruded on his shut-eye, Eric tried to block it out.

Maybe he shouldn't have succumbed when Kate insisted on taking the wheel for the final leg of their trip home, but tired as he was it had been safer. The four somewhat uncomfortable nights on the sofa bed in Cal's study, along with Caitlin's wee-hours fussiness, hadn't been conducive to restful sleep, and once darkness had fallen an hour ago his eyelids had grown heavy.

Turning over the wheel to Kate had made sense.

And he wasn't ready to wake up.

Yet hard as he tried to tune out the sound, it intensified.

Giving up his attempt to hang onto sleep, Eric opened his eyes and straightened up.

A few seconds later, the source of the sound became clear.

It was sleeting.

And given the sheen on the road, the icy pellets had been coming down for some time.

He looked over at Kate.

Despite the darkness that obscured her features, her rigid posture, fierce grip on the wheel, and intense focus on the road spelled tension in capital letters.

No surprise there.

This had to be a stark reminder of a similar night five years ago.

He needed to get her out from behind the wheel of the car. Fast.

"Kate." Though he spoke softly, she jumped as her gaze jerked toward his.

"You're awake." Her tight voice was edged with panic.

"How long has the weather been bad?"

"About half an hour."

"Why don't you pull onto the shoulder and let me take over?"

"It's too icy to stop here. And the shoulder's too narrow. There's a d-drop-off at the edge."

"There's plenty of room." He maintained a calm, reassuring tone. "Just take it slow and easy. There's no one behind us."

After a moment, she did as he instructed. Once she put the car in park, she released a long, shaky breath. "Sorry. I don't like driving in this kind of weather, but I d-didn't want to wake you."

"I'm awake now." Wide awake. "If you can slide over, I'll go around to the driver's side."

She nodded.

By the time he'd slipped and slid around the front of the car and settled himself behind the wheel, she was huddled into the corner of the passenger seat, the glow from the dome light illuminating her pallor and the thin film of perspiration beading on her upper lip. Her breathing was also shallow.

Frowning, he reached over and took her icy hand in his. "Everything's going to be fine. We're almost home. You'll be back in your apartment in less than an hour. Okay?"

Again, she bobbed her head.

For the next sixty minutes he gave the road his full attention. Because her concern—if not its intensity—was valid. The pavement was slick and hazardous, and conditions continued to worsen with every minute that passed.

Only when he pulled into a vacant spot in front of her apartment and shut off the engine did the knot in his stomach ease.

After taking a deep breath, he angled toward her. "We made it."

"Th-thank you for getting us here safely."

"Are we home?" Sarah spoke through a yawn from the back seat.

Eric turned, lightening his tone. "Indeed we are, Miss Sarah."

She rubbed her eyes and stared out the window. "Is it snowing?"

"Not yet. But it wouldn't surprise me if we woke up to a winter wonderland tomorrow. Right now it's just ice. And very slippery."

"Can I build a snowman tomorrow if it snows, Mommy?"

"We'll see." Kate's voice was laced with weariness.

"Sit tight." He opened his car door. "I'll take Sarah in and come back for you."

"I can manage." She released her seat belt.

He restrained her with a touch. "Humor me, please. I don't think we want any trips to the emergency room for broken bones on a night like this."

"I see your point." She reached for her purse and fumbled

inside for her keys. Handed them over. "Be careful."

"Always."

He opened his door. Stepped out.

The pavement was like a newly cleaned skating rink.

Moving with extreme caution, he circled behind the car, freed Sarah from the booster seat, and swung her into his arms. "Hold on tight, sweetie."

After tucking her against his chest, he shielded her face from the stinging sleet with his hand as he traversed the slick pavement.

Once he deposited her inside the small lobby of the apartment building, he returned for Kate.

She opened her door as he approached. "Is it as bad as it looks?"

"Worse. Let's take it slow and easy." He crooked his elbow as she stood.

She slipped her arm through his, then motioned to the trunk. "What about the luggage?"

"I'll come back for it after I get you inside."

Slowly they made their way to the door.

When she stepped inside, Kate released a shuddering breath. "I've never been in love with this apartment, but right now I could kiss the floor."

"You can do that in your unit while I get the luggage. I'd like to head home ASAP."

Her forehead knitted. "It's too dangerous to drive."

"I'll be careful. There aren't many cars on the street, so—"

"Why don't you stay with us tonight, Dr. Eric?" Sarah shifted her attention from him to Kate. "He could sleep on the sofa bed like you used to do before Grandma went to heaven."

Not a half-bad idea, given the dicey road conditions.

But he wasn't going to push.

Because unless Kate was comfortable with the notion of him sleeping under her roof, doing so would simply trade one slippery slope for another.

10

As the seconds ticked by while Eric and Sarah waited for her to respond, Kate tried to calm the flutter in her nerve endings.

There was no reason to be skittish about Eric spending the night. He was a gentleman through and through. And it was clearly the safest option.

Calling up a smile, she nodded. "That's a good idea. It's treacherous out there. Would you consider it?"

"Yes." No hesitation on Eric's part. "To tell you the truth, the thought of any further driving tonight is more than a little daunting."

"Understandable. I'll take Sarah up and make the sofa bed for you while you get our luggage."

"Sounds like a plan." He handed her the keys.

As he dived back into the storm, Kate took Sarah's hand and led her to the steps. Most days, she didn't even notice the climb to their second-floor apartment, but tonight her legs felt like lead.

Her white-knuckled time behind the wheel had taken a toll.

By the time they reached the apartment and she sent Sarah to her room to get ready for bed, even the task of making up the sofa bed felt overwhelming.

But she'd muscle through, as she always did.

However, when Eric reappeared a few minutes later, she'd

only managed to retrieve sheets and a blanket from the linen closet, thanks to her flagging energy.

"I was able to get all your luggage in one trip." He set their gear on the floor. "Once I grab my overnight bag we'll be set."

"Sounds good." She summoned up the hint of a smile.

After giving her a once-over, he crossed to the couch. "I'll open this for you first."

"I can manage, Eric. I did it every night for a long time."

"Not after driving through a bad storm. That was exhausting." Without pausing, he removed the cushions from the couch, set them against the wall, and opened the sofa bed. "I'll be back in a minute."

Once he exited, she shifted into a higher gear, and by the time he returned she had the bed half made. "I'm almost finished."

"No hurry on my end." He deposited his bag beside the others in the foyer.

"I'm ready for bed, Mommy." A pajama-clad Sarah trotted into the living room.

"I'll be ready to tuck you in in a few minutes, honey."

"Would you like me to take care of that?"

Before she could respond to Eric's question, Sarah spoke up. "Yes! Will you read me a story too?"

"A short one, if that's okay with your mommy."

Pressure built behind Kate's eyes as she bunched the edge of the pillow in her fingers.

Since Mom died, she'd been on her own for all the daily chores of life. Not that taking care of Sarah was a burden, but on nights like this, when fatigue weighed on her, a helping hand would have been welcome.

And if Eric was willing to step in, why not let him?

"Are you certain you don't mind?"

"Not in the least." He shifted toward Sarah and winked. "Lead the way, young lady."

As the two of them disappeared down the hall, Kate finished making the bed. But her mind wasn't on the rote task.

Instead, it was on the man who'd come so unexpectedly into her world. A man who was poised to play a huge role in her life— if she let him.

Except there really wasn't much doubt in her mind about that anymore. In truth, it was now a matter of when, not if.

She finished tucking in the blanket. Put the pillow in a fresh pillowcase and set it on the bed, her gaze drifting to the wedding photo of her and Jack on the side table.

Amy had been right. The man she'd loved wouldn't want her to spend the rest of her life alone.

It was time to move on.

She wandered into the kitchen to make a cup of tea, and when Eric reappeared a few minutes later she was taking her first sip.

"Three pages into the story, she was out like a light." He sent her a smile, but the grooves bracketing his mouth and the fan of lines at the corners of his eyes were silent evidence that the stress-ful drive had taken a toll on him too.

"Would you like a cup of decaf tea?" She hefted her mug.

"I'm more of a coffee guy in general, but I'll take you up on that tonight." He leaned back against the counter and folded his arms.

She filled another mug with hot water and put it in the mi-crowave. "I was planning to go in to say good night to Sarah, but if she's already asleep I don't want to wake her."

"I think she was worn out from the nonstop action at Amy's.

She was more than ready to crash. I think we all are. That was quite a drive."

"Tell me about it." She took a deep breath as she retrieved another teabag from the box. "You'd think by now I'd have gotten over my fear of being on the road in bad weather, but I can't seem to shake it. Even here in town I try to avoid driving when the roads are slick. Especially at night."

"It can take years for the kind of trauma you went through to dissipate. Cut yourself some slack."

In silence, she pulled two paper napkins from the cabinet. Set them on the table. "I wish I was as strong and resilient as Amy."

"Hey."

At his gentle summons, she looked over—and his tender expression jacked up her pulse.

He pushed off from the counter and slowly walked over to her, never breaking eye contact. "You *are* strong and resilient. Don't ever doubt that. You're also warm and compassionate and loving…and beautiful." He stopped inches away.

Somehow she found her voice. "No one's said that to me in a long time."

The microwave pinged.

She ignored it.

"Do you mind if I say it now?"

"No."

He lifted his hand. Cupped her cheek with his palm. "Is it okay if I do this?"

"Y-yes."

"How about this?" He bent down. Brushed his lips over hers, leaving a trail of fire in his wake.

Oh, mercy.

Her eyelids drifted closed.

"May I take that as a yes?" A hint of amusement lurked beneath the huskiness of his voice.

All she could do was nod.

He eased in, urging her closer, and she went without protest. And then he lowered his lips to hers for a real kiss.

A kiss that started off gentle and exploratory but quickly morphed to passionate when she responded fully.

A kiss that reflected pent-up longing and the wonder of discovery.

A kiss filled with promise and hope.

When he at last broke contact, his breathing was as ragged as hers.

"Wow." She tried to kick-start her lungs.

"Ditto."

"You know...I was afraid I'd be out of practice."

One side of his mouth quirked up. "Well, if you kiss like this when you're out of practice, I have serious concerns for my blood pressure once you're up to speed." He exhaled. "Why don't we take a break and have our tea?"

Smart idea. They both needed a chance to process what had just happened.

She pulled his mug from the microwave, added the tea bag, and joined him by the table. He waited until she sat, then took his own seat.

"I guess we crossed into new territory tonight, didn't we?" She grasped the handle of her mug. Held on tight.

"Yes. Are you having second thoughts?"

"No. This feels right to me. What about you?"

"The same."

"I still think we should be slow and cautious, though. Neither of us is in the market for more heartbreak."

"I'll drink to that." He lifted his mug.

She clinked hers with his.

And as they drank their tea while sleet coated the outside world with ice, warmth filled her heart.

For if all went well, maybe, just maybe, she wouldn't be spending the rest of her life alone.

* * *

There was nothing like waking up to the smell of brewing coffee—her morning beverage of choice.

And since the chore of making it fell to her these days, the heavenly aroma wafting into her bedroom must mean her unexpected houseguest was up.

Kate stretched. Smiled.

Maybe she hadn't had the most restful sleep after their kiss last night, but energy coursed through her.

"Knock knock. Are you decent?"

Her heart missed a beat at the question from a husky, very male voice.

She sat up, pulling the covers higher over her sleep shirt. "Yes."

Eric opened the door, a coffee mug in hand.

Sarah squeezed past him and plopped on the bed. "Hi, Mommy."

"Hi, honey. My goodness, you're dressed already."

"Dr. Eric helped me."

Lips twitching, he strolled across the room. "Someone was up with the chickens."

As she should have been, since it was a work day.

A zing of panic ricocheted through her. "Oh, no! I forgot to set the alarm last night. What time is it? I don't want to be late for school."

"You're a lady of leisure today. They declared a snow day."

She furrowed her brow. "They never do that. How bad is it out there?"

"Not good—but at least the ice has switched over to snow." He handed her the coffee.

"Thank you." She wrapped her fingers around the warm ceramic. "I'm not used to such service. Do you do windows?"

"Depends on what the job pays." His eyes began to twinkle.

She was saved from having to reply when Sarah spoke again. "Are you staying here all day, Dr. Eric?"

"I'd like to, but kids still get sick when it snows. I have to take care of them."

"I wish you didn't have to go out." Kate fought back another wave of panic. "What are the roads like?"

"Manageable in daylight. According to local media, the main routes are clear." He took her free hand. Gave it a squeeze. "I'll be careful. I promise." Then he turned to Sarah. "Do you think you could find a piece of paper and a pen for me in the kitchen, sweetie?"

"Uh-huh." She scooted off the bed and skipped down the hall.

As soon as she was out the door, Eric leaned down, the banked fire in his eyes igniting. "I couldn't leave without doing this." He closed the distance between them and claimed a kiss that was much too short. "I wish we had more time." His breath was warm on her cheek as he broke contact.

"There's always tonight."

"Is that an invitation?"

"Yes."

159

"I accept."

At the sound of running feet, he straightened up.

"Is this okay, Dr. Eric?" Sarah dashed in and held out a tablet and pen.

"That's perfect." Eric took it, scribbled something, and handed it across the bed.

She glanced at it.

Counting the hours.

She pressed it to her heart and looked up at him. "Me too."

"Get some rest today."

"I will."

But rest wasn't at the top of her agenda as he gave Sarah a hug and disappeared out the door.

She had another far more important chore to take care of before he returned tonight.

Unfortunately, it was afternoon before she got around to it—and only after she coaxed Sarah to take a much-needed nap on the heels of a snowman-building session.

But now she had the private window of time she needed.

After positioning a kitchen chair at the open door of her closet, she climbed onto the seat and withdrew the cherished box from the top shelf.

Cradling it in her arms, she carried it to the living room and set it on the couch. Sat beside it and opened the lid.

The contents were achingly familiar. The wedding invitation slotted into its cream-colored envelope. The program for the service, done in beautiful calligraphy. The place cards containing her name and Jack's. The ribbon from her wedding bouquet...and the rose she'd kept, once fresh and vibrant but now dried and lifeless.

She fingered a brittle petal as a pang echoed in her heart.

The flower was so representative of her life. Bright and fresh eleven years ago on her wedding day, dry and empty since Jack died.

Blinking away the mist in her vision, she set the rose aside and pulled out the album. Slowly paged through, memories of that happy day looping through her mind.

When she reached the last page—a close-up portrait of the two of them—she swallowed. Sniffed.

No one had ever touched her heart in quite the way Jack had, and no one had had his knack for helping her tap into her inner child.

He'd been one of a kind, and there would never be anyone like him again. Their time together—all the precious memories of the life they'd shared—belonged always to them.

But now it was time to make new memories with Eric. Create something that was theirs alone, separate and apart from her life with Jack. It was time to believe in tomorrow again. To embrace the sentiment that had been on the counted-cross-stitch sampler she'd worked on at Jack's bedside during the months he'd been in the extended-care facility.

A sampler she'd put aside and never finished when her hope dimmed.

But she still had it. Somewhere in her closet, most likely.

She repacked her box of wedding memories, picked up the photo from the side table, and returned to her bedroom.

After crawling into the farthest corners of her closet and rummaging around, she emerged with the dusty bag containing her unfinished embroidery.

Knees pulled up, back propped against the wall, she with-drew the piece of linen that was still taut in the hoop. Ran her fingers over the partially stitched words of hope for a future that was never meant to be.

Clutching it to her chest, she closed her eyes as a tear slipped past her lower lashes. "I love you, Jack." The whispered words rasped past her throat. "I always will. You filled my life with joy and beauty and laughter and sunshine. I'll never forget that. And I'll never let Sarah forget what a wonderful man you were."

The tear trailed down her cheek, and she reached up. Brushed it off. "But I still have a road to travel here, and I don't want to make the journey alone. So if all continues to go well with Eric and he asks me to marry him at some point, I'm going to accept. But I love you no less because I also love him."

She opened her eyes. Lifted the wedding photo. "Goodbye, my love. Until we meet again."

Then she gently tucked it into the box with the album, closed the lid, and returned her memories to the shelf in her closet—a much-cherished piece of her past but no longer an impediment to her future.

And after she did one last thing, she'd be ready to move forward.

Hopefully with a very special doctor by her side.

11

Her wedding ring was gone.

As Kate welcomed him at the door later that evening, Eric did a double take when her bare finger registered while she took his coat.

That was huge.

Before he could comment, Sarah bounded in from the living room. "Hi, Dr. Eric. Me and Mom built a snowman in the park today, with a carrot for a nose."

He switched gears, calling up a smile. "That sounds like fun."

"It was. And look at our new picture." She took his hand and tugged him into the living room. Pointed to a Monet print behind the couch.

"That's very pretty."

But his gaze homed in on the table where the wedding photo of Kate and Jack had once been displayed.

It was gone.

Also huge.

"I like it too." Sarah cocked her head as she studied the print. "It was in the hall closet. Mommy said it was too pretty to keep hidden away. And guess what we're going to put there?" She pointed to the empty spot on the table.

"I have no idea."

"A picture of you and me and Mom from Thanksgiving at Aunt Amy's. Mom said sometimes you have to put things away to make room for new things."

Eric turned to Kate, and when their gazes met her message was clear.

I'm ready to move on...with you.

"We're having chicken and dressing and biscuits tonight." Sarah hopped from one foot to the other. "And chocolate cake!"

"Sounds like a celebration." He kept his gaze on Kate.

A flush rose on her cheeks. "It is. Christmas is coming, after all—along with the start of a new year." She refocused on Sarah. "Honey, you have just enough time to finish watching your video before dinner."

"Okay." The little girl returned to the TV set and sat cross-legged in front.

"I have a few more things to do in the kitchen." Kate wiped her palms down her leggings.

"I'll lend a hand."

He followed her in but grabbed her hand and looped his arms around her waist once they were out of Sarah's sight. "I like the redecorating."

"It was time." Her voice was soft but certain. "I don't want to live in the past anymore. I'll never forget my life with Jack, and I'll always love him, but memories can only sustain you for so long. I want to feel like my life is rich and full and filled with promise again. To move forward and make new memories."

"I feel the same way. And I think you and Sarah and I could make beautiful memories together. I also think we can make this a Christmas to remember."

A slow smile curved her lips. "I like the sound of that."

"Then let's start making merry right now." He dipped his

head and claimed a kiss—which came to an abrupt end when Sarah bounded into the kitchen.

But that was okay.

Because if everything went as he hoped, there would be many more to come during the Christmas season—and in the years ahead.

* * *

This was turning out to be the best holiday she could remember in a very long time.

Thanks to Eric.

Lips flexing, Kate finished tucking Sarah into bed as the countdown toward Christmas accelerated.

Whether it was a simple dinner at her apartment, an impromptu meal out, a family outing with Sarah and Anna, or quietly sipping hot chocolate by the tree after Sarah went to bed, each moment with him was golden.

And as their relationship blossomed into romance, her life took on a new glow.

Even Sarah noticed, based on the out-of-the-blue question she asked as Kate tucked her in and sat beside her a week before Christmas.

"Are you going to marry Dr. Eric, Mommy?"

Kate froze.

She probably should have anticipated this moment, since she and Eric had begun to exchange more physical signs of affection in Sarah's presence. Now she'd have to wing it.

She smoothed out a wrinkle in the blanket. "He hasn't asked me to, honey."

"But what if he does?"

"What do *you* think I should do?"

Sarah considered her. "Would he live with us if you got married?"

"We'd all live together. At Dr. Eric's house, I expect."

"Would he be my daddy?"

That was a tougher question. It was critical to keep Jack's memory alive but also leave room for Eric.

"Actually, you'd have *two* daddies." She picked up the photo of Jack and Sarah from the nightstand as she formulated her answer. "When you were born, this was your daddy. He's in heaven now, so you can't see him, but he still loves you very much. And so does Dr. Eric. He'd be your daddy here. So you'd have a daddy in heaven and one here on earth."

Sarah studied her, expression solemn. "Do you still love my first daddy?"

"Of course. I always will. But he wouldn't want us to be lonesome. I think he'd be happy if Dr. Eric was part of our family since he can't be with us himself."

Sarah kneaded the edge of the sheet with her fingers. "I'd like to have a daddy I could see." After a few moments, her pensive expression morphed into a smile. "If Dr. Eric asks you to marry him, I think you should. Then we could be a real family. That would be my best Christmas present ever."

Hers too.

And as Kate kissed her daughter's forehead and turned out the light, hope for that very outcome burned bright in her heart.

* * *

"Kate? Eric. I've got a problem at the hospital."

Frowning, she glanced at her watch.

166

Sarah had to be at church in forty-five minutes for the Christmas pageant, and Eric had planned to take them.

"Will you be tied up long?"

"Possibly. I've got a little boy who was just diagnosed with meningitis."

Kate closed her eyes.

What a terrible thing for that child and his family to deal with during a season that was supposed to be joyous.

"I'm sorry. How old is he?"

"Seven. Even worse, he's an only child. The parents are panic-stricken."

"I can imagine. How bad is he?"

"Bad." The dire tone of his voice sent a shiver through her.

"Don't worry about tonight. I'll take Sarah. Maybe you can meet us there later if things improve."

A weary sigh came over the line. "I'm sorry about this. Sarah will be so disappointed."

That was true. Her daughter had been looking forward to having him and Anna in the audience. But an emergency took precedence.

"I'll explain it to her, Eric. Don't worry."

"I wish Mom hadn't agreed to go early to help set up refreshments. Otherwise you could have driven there together."

"We'll be fine. Just do what you can for that poor little boy and his parents."

"I will. And thank you for understanding. For not hating my work and resenting the disruptions it can cause." His voice roughened.

Mercy.

Living with Cindy must have been a constant source of stress, given the obligations and demands of his job.

She gentled her tone. "Eric, your profession is part of who you are. Your conscientiousness and caring are two of the things I lo—" She halted. Cleared her throat. "Things I respect in you and find appealing. So stop worrying and go do your job."

"You'll explain to Sarah? Tell her I'm sorry?"

"Yes. We'll see you later."

"Count on it."

As Kate ended the call, Sarah bounded into the kitchen, holding the wreath with her halo attached. "When do we have to leave, Mommy?"

"In about fifteen minutes." She sat and tugged Sarah onto her lap. "I just talked to Dr. Eric, honey. He's at the hospital with a very sick little boy. He has to stay and try to help him get better so he can go home for Christmas."

Her daughter's face fell. "But he was supposed to take us to church."

"I know. But we can go ourselves."

Sarah's lower lip began to quiver. "Isn't he even coming to see me in the Christmas pageant?"

"He's going to try his best, honey, but he isn't sure he'll be able to get there in time. If you were sick and had to go to the hospital and needed Dr. Eric, wouldn't you want him to stay with *you*?"

"Yes. But he said he'd come to my show. And I need him too."

"Dr. Eric knows that, and he asked me to tell you how sorry he is about this." She smoothed back a wisp of Sarah's hair. "When you're a doctor, though, sometimes other people need you more. This little boy is so sick that he might die if Dr. Eric doesn't stay with him."

Sarah's forehead crimped. "You mean like Daddy did?"

"Yes. And then his mommy and daddy would be all alone, just like we were after Daddy went to heaven."

"They'd be sad, wouldn't they? Like you used to be."

"Yes, they would."

Sarah dipped her chin, let out a shuddering sigh, and spoke in a small voice. "I guess maybe that boy does need Dr. Eric more than I do tonight."

Throat pinching, Kate gave her a squeeze. "I'm proud of you, honey. It's very grown-up to put other people first. And I know if there's any way Dr. Eric can get to your program, he will."

But he didn't.

Even worse, by the time the pageant ended a mixture of sleet and snow had begun to fall.

As she stood next to a window beside Anna after the program and watched the street disappear under a layer of white, Kate's stomach began to churn. "I'm going to head home, Anna." Hard as she tried to control her anxiety, a tremor crept into her voice. "I don't like driving in bad weather."

"I understand." Eric's mother patted her arm. "But you'll have to pry Sarah away from the dessert table."

Kate glanced at her daughter, who was eyeing the wonderland of sweets that was the centerpiece of the after-pageant social. "We'll make a plate to go. Will you be okay getting home?"

"No worries. I came with another member of the hospitality committee, and she has a four-wheel drive. In fact, if you want to wait, you could ride with us and leave your car here."

If only that was an option.

"I'd love to take you up on your offer, but I need my car for school tomorrow."

"Well, be very careful."

169

"I will."

By the time Kate buckled Sarah into the booster seat and slid behind the wheel, the icy mixture had intensified.

She checked on her daughter in the rearview mirror as she put the car in gear, but the weather hadn't phased Sarah, who was busy sampling her smorgasbord of desserts.

At least one of them was calm.

But with any luck, they'd be home long before Sarah made a dent in her plate of goodies.

* * *

Eric swung into the church parking lot, correcting his slight skid on autopilot.

In fact, he'd relied on autopilot during the entire drive from the hospital while his brain was consumed with second-guessing.

Was there anything else he could have done? Had he reacted quickly enough? Had he pushed the tests through as fast as possible? Would it have made any difference if they'd arrived at a diagnosis even half an hour sooner? Could he have found better words to comfort the parents of the child who'd died on his watch?

Eric parked. Set the brake. Took a long, unsteady breath as he trudged toward the church hall, the icy mixture stinging his cheeks.

Despite years of dealing with scenarios like this, he'd never learned to insulate himself from the pain. It always ripped through him like a knife, leaving his heart in shreds.

If he hadn't promised Kate he'd try to get here tonight, he'd have gone straight home and—

"Heavens, Eric. Are you all right?" Anna hurried over to him as he entered the hall, where the jovial atmosphere chafed his raw emotions like rubbing alcohol on a cut.

He jammed his hands into the pockets of his jacket. "Not especially."

His mother's features softened. "Kate told me about your patient. Did he…"

"He didn't make it."

Anna's irises began to glisten, and she touched his arm. "I'm so sorry. I know how losses like this tear you up."

"I'm in great shape compared to the parents."

"I know you did all you could. That's how you're wired."

He exhaled. Raked his fingers through his hair. "I hope so." He surveyed the room. "Is the pageant over?"

"Yes. Would you like some coffee?"

"No." Once more he scanned the room. "Where are Kate and Sarah?"

"They left about five minutes ago. Kate said she didn't want to stay for the social in case the weather got any worse. She seemed quite worried."

Of course she did.

It was sleeting out, just like it had been the night her husband was critically injured.

Like it had been on their drive back from Tennessee when she'd been terrified.

"I'll call you tomorrow, Mom." He tossed the promise over his shoulder while he jogged toward the door.

As he set off on the familiar route from the church to Kate's apartment, driving as fast as the deteriorating conditions allowed, his pulse accelerated. And until he confirmed she was safe, there was nothing he could do to slow it down.

A mile from her apartment, he finally caught sight of her car

171

creeping along the ice-covered street. She was being super cautious, but she was safe. In a couple of minutes he'd be behind her, and a few minutes after that, she'd be home.

Thank you, God.

Eric continued to close the distance between them as Kate stopped at an intersection. After a long pause, her car rolled on.

But fast-approaching headlights suddenly appeared on one of the cross streets. Brakes squealed. And then the other car slammed into the passenger side of Kate's vehicle.

For the second time in a handful of hours, Eric felt as if someone had plunged a knife into his gut.

In spite of the ice, he stepped on the accelerator, skidding to a stop with only inches to spare from the back of her car.

The other driver was already out of his vehicle and didn't seem to be injured.

"I tried to stop, but I kept sliding on the ice."

Eric was in no mood for excuses. "Call 911." As he barked out the order, he slipped and slid across the icy surface toward Kate's car.

He tried Sarah's door first, but it was too smashed to budge and he couldn't see inside, thanks to the icy coating on the window. But he could hear her crying.

Heart hammering, he circled the car and pulled open the driver's door.

Immediately the wrenching sound of Sarah's sobbing spilled out.

He bent down.

Kate was twisted sideways, frantically trying to reach her daughter's seat belt. But she was too constrained by her own to work the clasp.

Eric reached in and unsnapped her belt. "Kate, are you all right?"

If she heard him, she didn't respond. Instead, she tried to pivot onto her knees, never taking her focus off Sarah.

"Kate, look at me." He put his hands on her shoulders. "I need to know if you're all right."

She turned then, her eyes frantic. Dazed. When recognition dawned, her face crumpled. "It was sleeting. I was s-so afraid to drive." A tear slid down her cheek. "I n-needed you, and..." Her voice choked.

And he hadn't been there.

Because of his job.

The knife in his stomach twisted.

But he couldn't think about the ramifications of her words now.

"Are you hurt?"

"No. Just help Sarah."

"I will." He unlocked the back door and moved next to her. "Hey, Sarah. It's Dr. Eric. Can you look at me?"

Her sobbing abated a hair and she turned to him, eyes wide.

The dark splotches on her face triggered a spurt of adrenaline—until the plate of cake and cookies on the floor registered.

It wasn't blood.

It was chocolate.

Relief coursed through him.

"Sarah, sweetie, can you tell me what hurts?"

"M-my arm."

"I'm going to unbuckle your seat belt and take a look, okay?" He kept his voice calm and matter-of-fact, which required a yeoman effort.

"Where's Mommy?" Her lower lip began to quiver.

"I'm here, Sarah." Kate leaned around him so she could see her. "Just do what Dr. Eric says. Everything's okay." But her shaky voice said otherwise.

"Sarah, can you turn toward me? I want to take a look at your arm. I promise I'll try not to hurt you." Eric unsnapped her seat belt as he spoke, holding it away from her body as it slid into its holder.

She angled toward him, her sobs subsiding. While her down-filled parka had probably padded her somewhat from the impact, it also hampered his exam.

He reached over, unzipped her coat, and eased it off her shoulders. "It looks like you had chocolate cake tonight. Was it good?"

"Yes. But I didn't get to f-finish it." Her voice hiccupped.

"Well, we'll have to get you your very own cake to make up for that."

"Really?"

"Yep." He carefully pressed her arm in critical places through the thin knit of her sweater, gently manipulating it as he worked his way up. "Do you want chocolate or yellow?"

"Chocolate."

"A woman after my own heart. Chocolate or white icing?"

"Chocolate. And maybe it could have—ouch!" She gave a startled yelp when he reached her elbow.

"I'm sorry, sweetie. Does it hurt up here too?" He pressed along her upper arm to her shoulder.

"No."

"Is anyone here injured?"

At the question, Eric shifted around to find a police officer leaning into the car behind him. "Nothing too serious, as far as I can tell. I'm a doctor."

"Should I call an ambulance?"

That would only upset Kate and Sarah even more—but it wasn't his choice to make.

He turned to Kate. "I don't think there are any acute injuries, but Sarah should be seen at an ER. I can take you if you prefer."

"We'll go with you."

"We'll have the car towed and send someone to the hospital to get a statement." The officer angled away from the sleet. "Where are you taking her?"

After Eric gave him that information, he turned back to Sarah and draped the parka over her shoulders. "I don't want to hurt your arm. Can you scoot over and put your other arm around my neck?"

She complied, and a moment later he eased out of the car with her in his arms.

"You'll be okay, honey." Kate touched her daughter's cheek, the lines of strain in her face accentuated by the flashing police lights.

"You should get checked out too." He put a protective hand over Sarah's face as sleet continued to ping around them.

"No." Kate shook her head. "Let's focus on her. I'm fine."

She didn't look fine. Her face was colorless and she was shaking. But he wasn't about to linger in this icy bombardment and argue.

"Hold on to my arm. I'm parked right behind you."

Within three minutes they were on their way to the hospital, Kate in the back seat with Sarah. Though he tried again during the drive to convince her to be examined, she refused.

"I'm not hurt. Just shaken up. I'll feel better when I know for sure that Sarah is all right."

Which she was, except for a bruised elbow, based on a thorough exam.

Kate's shoulders sagged when he gave her the good news, and a tear spilled out of her eye. "Thank God."

It took every ounce of his willpower to resist the powerful urge to take her in his arms and comfort her.

But that sort of response was no longer appropriate.

Not after what she'd said at the accident scene.

While her words had been spoken in the midst of trauma, during a moment of panic and fear, they'd seared themselves into his soul.

"I needed you."

And though she hadn't said anything else, the implication had been clear.

At a critical moment in her life, he hadn't been there.

It was an echo of Cindy's oft-repeated message.

"You're never there when I need you."

And Cindy had been right—just as Kate had been right a couple of hours before.

If he'd attended the pageant, as he'd promised, the accident would never have happened. They would have stayed for the social, and they would never have crossed paths with the other driver.

Once again, his profession had gotten in the way of his private life—with consequences that could have been far worse.

And it could very well happen again.

Which led him back to the disheartening conclusion he'd reached long ago.

Marriage and medicine didn't mix.

12

Eric was slipping away from her.

And she didn't have a clue why.

Biting her lip, Kate stared out the window at the leaden skies and the barren trees cloaked in a dull, gray fog. *Everything* was gray—including the future that had seemed so golden until the accident four days ago.

It wasn't as if Eric had disappeared from their life. He'd brought Sarah her own miniature chocolate cake, as he'd promised, and he checked in every day to see how she was doing. He returned her texts and hadn't canceled their Christmas plans with Anna.

But the vibe between them was different. *He* was different. A polite stranger instead of the warm, caring man who'd kissed her with such passion.

And he wouldn't talk about it. Whenever she broached the subject, he simply said he was busy at work. Which did nothing to ease her mind.

She twisted her hands together and began to pace.

If she didn't do *something*, she was going to lose him. And she couldn't let that happen. Not without a fight. But how did you fight an unknown enemy? How did you tackle a phantom, a shadow?

No answer came to her.

But maybe a chat with Amy would help shed some light on the subject.

She veered over to the counter, picked up her cell, and tapped in her sister's number.

"Kate! This is a surprise. Tell me you changed your mind and decided to come down for Christmas. We'd love to host you and Sarah—and that hardworking doctor if he can spare the time off."

She dropped onto the couch. Rested her head against the cushioned back and stared at the water mark on the ceiling that the owner had been promising to fix since the day they moved in. "Right now he can't even spare the time to visit *me*."

"Is he super busy at work?"

"So he claims."

A beat ticked by. "Did you two have a falling out?"

"Not that I'm aware of, but ever since the accident, he—"

"Whoa! Back up! What accident?"

Whoops.

She'd been so distracted by Eric's switch from passionate to polite that she hadn't thought to tell Amy about the crash.

"Sorry. Some guy ran into our car the other night on the way back from the Christmas pageant. It was sleeting, and he lost control."

"Are you and Sarah all right?"

"Her elbow is bruised, but it's nothing serious. I wasn't injured."

"How's Eric?"

She frowned. "Fine. Why?"

"Didn't you tell me he was going to drive you that night?"

Right. She'd passed on that tidbit at some point.

"Yes, but he was delayed at the hospital. By the time he got to church we'd left, so he followed us. He was right behind us when the accident happened."

"You mean he witnessed the crash?"

"Yes."

A beat ticked by.

"Is that when things changed between the two of you?"

"Yes."

"Maybe he's just upset, Kate. Watching something like that unfold in front of your eyes, seeing people you care about in danger and not being able to do anything about it, could shake a person up."

"I know. And to make matters worse, he'd just lost a patient." Kate briefed her on the little boy with meningitis.

"That's so sad." Amy's voice was laced with compassion. "Having met Eric, I imagine he was devastated."

"Yes, he was." That had become clear as her nerves calmed and she'd asked him about the boy while they were at the hospital with Sarah.

"So let's try to piece this together. He'd had a terrible day. Then he disappointed Sarah, who was looking forward to having him at the pageant, and he had to renege on his promise to drive you to church. He also had problems in his first marriage because of conflicts between his career and personal life. Right?"

"Yes."

"Could those old fears be resurfacing? I can't get in his head, but maybe he figured that if he'd taken you to the pageant the accident might never have happened. He might have concluded that once again his job got in the way of his relationships, and he's backing off."

Amy's analytical skills were sharp as ever. "You may be right."

179

"Is it possible he thinks you're upset because he didn't make the pageant? That you blame him for what happened?"

Kate frowned. "Why would he think that? It wasn't his fault."

"Did you tell him that?"

Kate squinted at the water stain.

No, she hadn't.

In fact, what *had* she said to him when he'd arrived at the accident scene?

Closing her eyes, she dug deep into her memory banks.

She'd talked about not wanting to drive on the ice, that much she remembered. And she'd said something about how much she needed him, and how relieved she was to see him.

No. Wait.

She hadn't gotten to the part about being relieved. She'd just said she needed him, and then her voice had choked. All he'd heard was needed.

Past tense.

As in, "I needed you, and you weren't there." When what she'd intended to say was, "I needed you, and here you are."

Her stomach began to roil.

"Kate?"

At Amy's prompt, she straightened up. Wrapped her free arm around her middle. "I'm here. I just...I'm remembering fragments of our conversation when Eric arrived at the accident scene. I think I...that I inadvertently implied he'd let us down."

"Ouch. That could have played into the guilt he had to already be feeling about missing the event because of a conflict between his job and his personal life."

"Tell me about it." She leaned forward, fighting back a wave of nausea. "No wonder he pulled back. He had enough guilt laid on him in his first marriage to last a lifetime. He's not going to put himself in that position again."

"Look, this doesn't have to derail your romance."

"But I can't take back those words. And he isn't likely to forget them. No matter how hard I try to explain what I meant to say, he may not buy it."

"I agree that words may not be sufficient. I think this calls for action." A beat ticked by. "Do you love him enough to do something totally out of character?"

A tinge of unease rippled through her. "Like what?"

"Just answer the question."

Kate scrubbed a hand down her face.

She wasn't going to be comfortable with whatever Amy had in mind. Guaranteed. But her sister never gave bad advice.

Squaring her shoulders, she sat up straighter. "Yes."

"Do you think he loves you?"

"Yes."

"Then I have a plan."

* * *

Why was Kate's car parked in front of his mother's house?

Eric pulled into the driveway and set the brake.

The arrangement had been for him and Anna to pick up Kate and Sarah later for the Christmas Eve service, then spend the day together tomorrow.

It was going to be awkward, but Sarah was looking forward to him and Mom being part of her holiday, and it wasn't fair to disappoint her. Otherwise, he'd have had a long talk with Kate already.

Not that he wanted to cut things off with her, but what choice did he have? Hard as he'd tried to convince himself that he could balance career and family, and despite his belief that Kate would be able to live with the demands of his profession, the night of the accident had said otherwise.

She might not recall her words in that moment of crisis, but he would never be able to forget them. And people often said what was in their heart at emotional times like that.

On top of that, he'd let Sarah down by not being there for her Christmas program.

If he could promise them both he'd never disappoint them like that again, he'd do it in a heartbeat.

But short of changing careers, he couldn't give them that assurance. The truth was it *would* happen again. And again. And again. Until finally Kate grew disillusioned and bitter, as Cindy had.

He couldn't do that to her.

Or to himself.

Fighting back a wave of despair, he slid from behind the wheel and trekked toward the front door. For everyone's sake he needed to be upbeat, even if getting through the next thirty-six hours with even a semblance of holiday cheer would tax his acting skills to the limit.

The fragrant smell of pine mingling with the aroma of freshly baked cookies greeted him as he stepped inside the door, and a few moments later his mom appeared from the back of the house.

"Merry Christmas." She beamed him a smile.

"Same to you." He bent and kissed her cheek. "I was surprised to see Kate's car out front. I thought we were picking them up for services later."

"We were supposed to, but when I talked to her earlier she

didn't have any special dinner plans for Christmas Eve. So I invited them to come over early. I baked a ham, and there's plenty for two more. I didn't think you'd mind."

He should have alerted his mother that he was on the verge of stepping back from Kate. But he hadn't wanted to ruin *her* Christmas too.

Now he was stuck.

"Hi, Dr. Eric!" Sarah dashed into the hallway and launched herself at him.

He reached down and swept her up in his arms. "Hi, sweetie. How's that elbow?"

"It's kind of purple, but it doesn't hurt too much."

"Sarah, honey, are you ready to decorate the next batch of cookies?" Anna wiped her hands on her elf-themed apron.

"Yes. Do you want a cookie, Dr. Eric? Aunt Anna made them, and I decorated them."

"I'll have one a little later." He set her down, and as she scampered back to the kitchen he spoke to his mother again. "Where's Kate?"

"Right here." She appeared behind Mom, her face a tad flushed. "Do you all mind if I take a short walk? I love this crisp weather, and I feel a touch of snow in the air. It's very Christmasy out there."

Mom frowned. "It will be dark soon. I'm not crazy about you walking alone."

"I'll be fine." She crossed to the hall closet and retrieved her coat. "I won't be gone long. I only plan to walk to the park and back. And I'll take my cell." She picked up her tote bag from the chair in the foyer.

"Eric, why don't you go with her?" Anna nudged him.

He took a steadying breath.

Bad idea.

Spending time alone with her would be dangerous. It could undermine his determination to keep his distance.

But while Mom's neighborhood was safe, in this day and age it was dangerous for a woman to walk alone anywhere in the dark, even on Christmas Eve.

And if anything happened to Kate, he'd never forgive himself.

He took a slow breath and bit the bullet. "Unless you prefer a solo walk, why don't I go with you?"

"Two is always better than one." She smiled at him and pulled on her gloves.

"We'll be back soon, Mom." He opened the front door and moved aside as Kate walked past, the faint, pleasing fragrance that always emanated from her drifting through the air in her wake.

"Don't hurry. We won't eat for at least an hour. Have fun."

Not likely.

Kate waited while he shut the door, then fell into step beside him as they walked down the sidewalk and strolled toward the park at the corner.

Dusk was just beginning to fall, and the lights from Christmas trees twinkled in the windows they passed. With few cars out and about, the evening was still and peaceful.

"I've always loved Christmas Eve." Frosty clouds appeared in front of Kate's face as she spoke. "When I was a child, it was filled with such wonder and hope and anticipation. As if great, exciting things were about to happen. Was it like that for you?"

Eric shoved his hands into the pockets of his overcoat. "Yes. Thanks to Mom and Dad, it was a magical season. They made me feel that anything was possible." He clenched his fingers into a tight ball. "It's a shame we have to grow up and lose that belief in endless possibilities."

"Maybe we don't."

He let that pass, and they continued in silence.

Just as they reached the park, a few large, feathery flakes began to drift down, and somewhere in the distance carolers launched into "Silent Night."

"My favorite Christmas song." Kate paused, her mouth curving into a sweet smile. "Could we sit for a minute?" She motioned toward a park bench tucked between two fir trees bedecked with twinkling white lights.

Eric stifled a groan.

Sitting beside her, where the shimmering lights would add a luster to her ebony hair and a sparkle to her eyes, was playing with fire.

"We should probably go back. It's getting dark. And colder."

"I'm not cold. But if you are, I can stay for a few minutes on my own. I'm sure your mother's worries about safety are overblown."

Yes, they were.

But bad things happened everywhere, and there was no way he was leaving Kate alone in the dark.

"I'll stay with you."

She rewarded him with a smile, then led the way to the bench, set her tote bag on one end, and sat in the middle.

Not good.

He claimed the other end, keeping as much distance between them as possible, but she was still too close.

And as they listened to the distant, melodic voices, he couldn't help watching out of the corner of his eye as the falling snowflakes clung to her hair like gossamer stars.

It was the longest song of his life as he battled the impulse to touch her, calling on every ounce of his waning self-control to keep his hands to himself.

When the music ended at last, he started to rise—but she reached over and grasped his hand. "Can you give me another couple of minutes?" Her question came out a bit breathless, and a sudden, nervous energy crackled in the air.

As a *Proceed with Caution* sign began to flash in his mind, he sank back down. Angled toward her. "Okay."

"I want to talk about what happened the night of the accident."

So did he. But not on Christmas Eve.

"I agree we need to discuss that. But why don't we put it on hold until after—"

"No." She locked onto his gaze. "My life has been on hold too long." She turned toward the tote bag, withdrew a flat rectangular package, and held it out to him. "Let's start with this."

He stared at the gift wrapped in silver paper. "I thought we were exchanging presents tomorrow."

"This one's special. And private."

He hesitated, but after a moment he took the package, tore off the wrapping, and lifted the lid of the shallow box.

Inside was what looked like a hand-stitched sampler.

He angled it toward the light from the trees as he read the words from Robert Browning that were surrounded by a sunny, verdant garden filled with the promise of spring.

The best is yet to be.

"I started working on that when Jack was in the hospital." Kate's voice was quiet now. "It helped me hold onto the hope that things would get better, that our best years were still ahead. But when Jack died, I put it away. The words seemed to mock me rather than comfort. All I could see in my future was an endless string of dark days—until you came along and helped me realize it was time to tie up the loose threads and move on. So I did, literally and figuratively. You gave me the courage to start living again."

"I also let you down." His voice scratched, and he dipped his chin as the world around him blurred. "If I'd driven you to church, the accident would never have happened. But I can't change the nature of my job. And I can't promise what happened four days ago won't happen again, because it will."

"I know that. I understand the responsibilities that go with your job."

"But they wear on a relationship. They lead to resentment—and worse."

"Not for me. On the contrary. I respect you for being such a conscientious doctor. I may be disappointed sometimes if your duties take you away from us, but I know you'll always do your best not to let us down. And I'd never expect anyone to do more than their best."

As the snow continued to drift softly around them, Eric searched her eyes. Found only sincerity and a warmth that shot straight to his core.

What had he ever done to deserve a woman with such an understanding heart, and an inner beauty that surpassed even her physical loveliness?

An ember of hope ignited in his heart.

"I'd like to believe we could have a future together."

"That's why I want you to have the sampler. I hope it makes you think of the two of us every time you see it." She took a deep breath. "And now I'm about to do something very bold and out of character." She reached into her bag again, this time withdrawing a smaller, square box. When she handed it to him, her fingers were trembling.

His weren't much steadier as he unwrapped the second package and lifted the lid.

Inside, nestled on a bed of tissue, lay a delicate, heart-shaped blown-glass ornament with a loop of green satin ribbon at the top anchored with sprigs of holly.

"That gift is symbolic, Eric." Her voice wobbled, and she clenched her fingers together in her lap. "It represents my heart, which is yours if you want it. Forever. Because I love you, and I can't imagine my future without you. So if you're in the market for a wife, I'd like to apply for the job."

As her words registered, joy bubbled up inside him.

Unless he was misunderstanding her, his greatest Christmas wish had just come true.

"Did you just propose to me?"

Even in the dim light, there was no missing the surge of color on her cheeks.

"Yes. I realize this isn't the conventional approach, but I didn't know how else to convince you how much I love you. If you need to think about it, we can—"

"Wait. I don't need to think about it. I love you too, with every fiber of my being. And I can't imagine my life without you, either. But I come with liabilities, Kate. Ones that can undermine a relationship."

"They can't undermine a relationship built on a solid foundation, where both people understand and accept that their love is worth any trade-offs or sacrifices required. And as far as I'm concerned, your assets far outweigh your liabilities. You're kind and caring and generous and honorable and trustworthy—and you'll be a wonderful father to Sarah."

The taut muscles in his shoulders relaxed, and he laced his fingers with hers. Smiled. "In your litany of attributes, you forgot one thing."

"What?"

"I'm a great kisser."

A chuckle spilled out of her mouth. "That too. Although I haven't had any proof of that lately."

"Easy to remedy." He set the ornament aside and tugged her close.

She came without protest, wrapping her arms around his neck as he bent to claim her lips.

And as they kissed amid the snow and twinkle lights, the distant voices of the carolers once again broke into song, jubilantly proclaiming, "Joy to the World."

How perfect was that?

Epilogue

Five months later

I t was a beautiful day for a wedding.
Kate smiled and filled her lungs with the fresh mountain air as she gazed out the window of Amy's cabin.

New green shoots decorated the tips of the spruce trees, and the masses of rhododendrons and mountain laurel on the hillsides were laden with pink-hued blossoms. A kaleidoscope of yellow swallowtail butterflies fluttered by, undulating playfully in the warm afternoon sun, while classical flute music played a duet with the splashing water from the nearby stream.

The setting was peace personified. And symbolic.

For the rebirth of nature after a long, cold winter was like the new life she and Eric would start in a few minutes after their own long, cold winter of the heart.

"You look happy."

As Amy spoke, Kate turned. Her sister stood in the doorway with Sarah, holding two bouquets of roses, baby's breath and greenery.

"I am."

"And beautiful."

Kate angled toward the full-length mirror beside her and examined her reflection. The simple but elegant cut of her deep blue tea-length gown *was* flattering, and the overlay of delicate chiffon that swirled at the hem when she moved added a graceful touch.

"I have to admit I *feel* beautiful." And young. And breathless. And hopeful. And all the things every bride should feel on her special day.

"Do I look pretty too, Mommy?"

Smiling, Kate turned to her daughter. In her white eyelet dress, holding a basket of flowers, Sarah would fit in at a Victorian garden party.

"Yes, you do. The prettiest flower girl ever." Kate knelt and pulled her close. How blessed she'd been to have this precious child's unconditional love, sunny disposition, and innocent laughter to buoy her in the months following Jack's death and add joy to all her days. "And I love you with all my heart."

"I love you too." Sarah squirmed free and pointed to a bluebell tucked into her basket. "I picked that flower for Papa Eric before I got dressed. Aunt Amy says I can give it to him later."

"I'm sure he'll like that. It's the color of his eyes."

"If you two ladies are ready, I don't think we should keep the groom waiting any longer." Amy motioned toward the door of the bedroom.

Kate gave Sarah one more quick hug, then rose.

Holding out one of the bouquets, Amy crossed the room, her features soft with love. "You know how happy I am for you, don't you?"

"I know." She took the flowers, swallowing past the clog in her throat. "And thank you for everything. For your love and support and for always being there. You and Mom were my lifeline for so many years."

Amy's own voice was none too steady when she replied.

"And I always will be. But I'm more than happy to share that role with Eric."

The flute music changed to the hymn they'd chosen for the opening of the ceremony, and Kate's pulse picked up.

"It's time." Amy took Sarah's hand and led her down the steps and over to the door while Kate followed.

Sarah went first, and then Amy walked down the aisle and took her place as matron of honor beside the rose-bedecked arbor in front of the chairs that had been set up for the small, intimate wedding.

Kate drew a deep breath and stepped into the sunshine to make her own walk down the aisle.

Of course she noticed a few of the guests. A beaming Anna. Cal, who was juggling Caitlin in one arm while the twins beside him stared wide-eyed at the proceedings. Frank, up front as best man while his wife snapped photos.

But her focus was on Eric as he waited for her in the meadow with the blue-hazed mountains as a backdrop.

How handsome he was in the dove-gray suit that hugged his broad shoulders, the early afternoon sun turning his blond hair to gold. But it was his face that drew—and held—her gaze. It was strong and compassionate and caring, and his eyes spoke more eloquently than words of the passion and love and commitment in his heart.

And for all of her days, she'd give thanks for a second chance at love with this special man.

As she took her place beside him and the pure notes of "Joyful, Joyful, We Adore Thee" drifted through the mountain air, the appropriateness of the hymn resonated with her even more than the day they'd chosen it.

For with God's grace, the clouds of sadness and the dark of

doubt had melted away. And going forward, she and Eric would build on that grace, filling their days with joy and hope and light. Through all the seasons of their life.

**Keep reading for a preview of
THE BEST GIFT,
Book 1 in the Legacy of Love series.**

The Best Gift

LEGACY OF LOVE—BOOK 1
ENCORE EDITION

Prologue

"How much longer is he going to make us wait for the reading of the will? I have a plane to catch."

As her sister huffed out a breath, AJ Williams gave the flame-red maples one last scan through the window and turned away from the brilliant St. Louis late-October sky. "Chill out, Morgan. The advertising world will survive without you for a few more hours."

The corners of Morgan's lips dipped south. "Trust me, AJ. The business arena is nothing like your nonprofit world. Hours matter to us. So do minutes." She went back to scrolling on her cell.

"More's the pity. Life is too short to get stressed about something as fleeting as an ad campaign."

"Those ad campaigns pay the bills, and—"

"Morgan. AJ." Their older sister sent them each a gently chiding look. "Don't you think we should put our philosophical differences aside today, out of respect for Aunt Jo?"

AJ's mouth quirked. "Ever the peacemaker, Clare."

"Somebody had to be the referee between you two redheads while we were growing up."

"I'll call a truce if Morgan will." AJ arched an eyebrow at their middle sister.

Morgan tucked her cell back in her purse. "I'm in. Besides, much as I hate to admit that my kid sister is right, I do sometimes take my job too seriously."

AJ snorted. "Sometimes?"

"Hey. Let's not break the truce already." Clare's lips twitched.

"You win." AJ threw up her hands. "We'll be good. All I can say is you must whip those kids into shape when you substitute teach. In a nice way, of course. I bet their regular teacher is astounded at their good behavior when she gets back."

Twin lines creased Clare's brow. "I do my best, but it's been years since I taught, and some days are h-harder than others."

At the catch in her voice, Morgan moved beside her and took her hand. "Hang in there, okay? And remember, we're always here for you."

"I'll second that." AJ walked over too and pulled Clare into a hug. "And it does get easier. Not overnight, but bit by bit. Trust me." Her voice shook on the last couple of words, and she swallowed. Blinked to clear her vision. If she'd survived her own tragedy, Clare would too. The Williams women were strong.

Clare swiped a finger under her lashes and called up a shaky smile. "Sorry. I guess Aunt Jo's memorial service this morning brought a lot of emotions to the—"

The door to the office opened, and all three of them turned toward it as Seth Mitchell appeared on the threshold.

The distinguished, gray-haired attorney paused to give each of them an unhurried appraisal with his astute eyes.

AJ shifted her weight from one foot to the other under his scrutiny.

The man's expression didn't offer any clues to his thoughts, but he was no doubt impressed by her sisters. Who wouldn't be? She gave them a survey.

Morgan's dark, copper-colored hair was cut in a sleek, shoulder-length style, and her business attire spelled "big city" and "success" in capital letters. Clare was class personified with her honey-gold hair coiffed in an elegant chignon that was a perfect complement to her designer suit and Gucci purse.

AJ tucked a rebellious strand of her long, naturally curly strawberry blond hair behind her ear and smoothed a hand down the tunic top she'd cinched at the waist with a retro metal belt from a thrift shop. Same shop where she'd found the calf-length skirt that completed her eclectic outfit.

But if Aunt Jo's attorney was less than impressed by the youngest sister who marched to the beat of her own drummer, he gave no indication of it.

"Good morning, ladies." He moved into the room. "I'm Seth Mitchell. I recognize you from Jo's description—AJ, Morgan, Clare." He extended his hand to each in turn. "Please accept my condolences on the loss of your great-aunt. She was a wonderful lady."

"She was one of a kind." AJ's mouth quirked up.

The attorney flashed her an answering smile. "That she was. Why don't we all take seats, and I'll proceed with the reading of the will." He motioned to a conference table off to the side.

As they claimed chairs, he detoured to his desk and retrieved a hefty document before joining them. "I'll give each of you a copy of your great-aunt's will to take with you, so I don't think there's any reason to go through all of this now. A lot of it is legalese, and there are some minor charitable bequests that you can review at your leisure. I would suggest we restrict the formal reading to the section that affects each of you directly, if that's agreeable."

"Yes." Morgan answered for all of them. "My plane for Boston leaves in less than three hours. I know Clare needs to get back to Kansas City, and AJ has a long drive to Chicago."

"I'm glad we're in agreement. Otherwise, this would be a marathon session." Seth flipped through the document to a marked page and began to read. "Insofar as I have no living relatives other than my three great-nieces—the daughters of my sole nephew, Jonathan Williams, now deceased—I bequeath the bulk of my estate to them, in the following manner and with the following stipulations and conditions.

"To Abigail Jeanette Williams, I bequeath half ownership of my bookshop in St. Louis, Turning Leaves, with the stipulation that she retain ownership for a minimum of six months and work full-time in the store during this period. The remaining half ownership I bequeath to the present manager, Blake Sullivan, with the same stipulation.

"To Morgan Williams, I bequeath half ownership of Serenity Point, my cottage in Seaside, Maine, providing that she retains her ownership for a six-month period following my death and that she spends a total of four weeks in residence at the cottage during this time. She is also to provide advertising and promotional assistance for Good Shepherd Camp and attend board meetings as an advisory member. The remaining half ownership of the cottage I bequeath to Grant Kincaid of Seaside, Maine.

"To Clare Randall, I bequeath my remaining financial assets, except for those designated to be given to the charities specified in this document, with the stipulation that she serve as nanny for

Nicole Wright, daughter of Dr. Adam Wright of Hope Creek, North Carolina, for a period of six months, at no charge to Dr. Wright.

"Should the stipulations and conditions for the aforementioned bequests not be fulfilled, these assets will be disposed of according to directions given to my attorney, Seth Mitchell. He will also designate the date on which the clock will begin ticking on the six-month period specified in my will."

The lawyer lowered the document to his desk. "I can provide more details on your bequests to each of you individually, but are there any general questions?"

AJ checked on her sisters.

Morgan looked aggravated. Clare seemed confused.

"I may as well write mine off right now." Morgan expelled a breath. "There's no way I can be away from the office for four days, let alone four weeks. And what is Good Shepherd Camp?"

As the attorney answered her sisters' questions, AJ tuned out the exchange.

As far as she was concerned, this was going to be a grand adventure. One that was perfectly timed. Who could have guessed that just when she was ready for a change, a new challenge would drop into her lap? It had to be fate. Maybe she wasn't all that thrilled about sharing her adventure with this Blake whatever-his-name-was, but she'd go with the flow, like she always did. Everything would work out fine.

When her sisters finally stopped peppering Seth Mitchell with questions, he turned to her. "What about you, AJ? Is there anything you'd like to know?"

"Yes. When can I start at the bookshop?"

"I need a couple of weeks to tie up legalities before you contact Mr. Sullivan. I'll let you know when it's appropriate to call him." He pulled up the calendar on his phone. "Let's start the clock on the six-month period December 1. That will give you all about a month to make plans. Is that acceptable?"

"That works for me." AJ eyed her sisters, neither of whom seemed half as excited as she was about their bequests from Aunt Jo. "You two okay with that?"

Clare shrugged. "I guess so."

"Whatever." Morgan checked her watch.

"Then December 1 it is." The attorney handed them each a manila envelope. "Feel free to call if any questions come up as you review the will in more detail." He rose, and AJ stood along with her sisters. "Again, my condolences on the death of your great-aunt. Jo had a positive impact on countless lives and will be missed by many people. I know she loved each of you very much, and that she wanted you to succeed in claiming your bequests." He ushered them to the door. "Good luck, ladies."

AJ fell in behind her sisters as they exited, lips bowing while they filed through the plush outer office.

Morgan and Clare might have reservations about the feasibility of meeting the stipulations in Aunt Jo's will, but she had no such concerns about claiming her inheritance.

After all, how hard could it be to run a bookshop with this Blake guy for a mere six months?

This was going to be a piece of cake.

1

It wasn't fair.

Blake Sullivan stared at the letter from Seth Mitchell. Read it through again.

How could Jo do this to him? The bookshop was supposed to go to him.

Jamming his fingers through his hair, he began to pace in his foyer, where he'd stopped to open the official-looking letter after retrieving his mail.

Maybe Jo had never promised to leave the entire business to him in so many words, but she'd implied as much on multiple occasions since he'd taken the helm three years ago. Plus, they'd been close friends for twenty-one years. In fact, had it not been for that friendship, he would never have walked away from a successful career in investment banking to rescue Turning Leaves. But what else could he do, after it had become apparent that Jo's waning energy was having a negative impact on the business and that her legendary generosity had finally depleted her financial cushion?

He paused. Massaged his forehead.

Who knew he'd end up enjoying the business so much that he'd stay to not only get the shop back on solid financial ground but turn the sleepy, neighborhood bookstore into a thriving enterprise?

Heck, without him, the business would have been bankrupt by now.

And what was his reward for three years of diligent labor on Jo's behalf?

She'd left half the business to her flighty, do-gooder great-niece who probably didn't know the difference between a balance sheet and a balance beam.

Chill, Sullivan. Getting worked up about this isn't going to change anything.

That was true.

He took a deep breath. Exhaled. Repeated that exercise.

Better.

And maybe there was an explanation in the letter Mitchell had included, the envelope addressed to him in Jo's flowing hand.

Blake continued to the kitchen, slit the flap on the envelope with a knife, and pulled out the single sheet of paper.

Leaning against the countertop, he scanned the short note.

About the Author

© DeWeesePhotography.com

Irene Hannon is the bestselling, award-winning author of more than sixty-five contemporary romance and romantic suspense novels. She is also a three-time winner of the RITA award—the "Oscar" of romance fiction—from Romance Writers of America, and a member of that organization's elite Hall of Fame.

Her many other awards include National Readers' Choice, Daphne du Maurier, Retailers' Choice, Booksellers' Best, Carol, and Reviewer's Choice from *RT Book Reviews* magazine, which also honored her with a Career Achievement award for her entire body of work. In addition, she is a HOLT medallion winner and a two-time Christy award finalist.

Millions of copies of her books have been sold worldwide, and her novels have been translated into multiple languages.

Irene, who holds a BA in psychology and an MA in journalism, juggled two careers for many years until she gave up her executive corporate communications position with a Fortune 500 company to write full-time. She is happy to say she has no regrets.

A trained vocalist, Irene has sung the leading role in numerous community musical theater productions and is a soloist at her church. She and her husband enjoy traveling, hiking, gardening, and spending time with family. They make their home in Missouri.

To learn more about Irene and her books, visit www.irenehannon.com. She loves to interact with readers on Facebook and is also active on Instagram.

Made in the USA
Middletown, DE
12 January 2025

69360888R00125